Driftwood

Published in Canada by Fitzhenry & Whiteside,
195 Allstate Parkway, Markham, Ontario L3R 4T8

Published in the United States in 2013 by Fitzhenry & Whiteside, 311
Washington Street, Brighton, Massachusetts 02135

www.fitzhenry.ca   godwit@fitzhenry.ca

10 9 8 7 6 5 4 3 2 1

Library and Archives Canada Cataloguing in Publication
Driftwood
ISBN 978-1-55455-305-1
Data available on file

Publisher Cataloging-in-Publication Data (U.S.)
Driftwood
ISBN 978-1-55455-305-1
Data available on file

Fitzhenry & Whiteside acknowledges with thanks the
Canada Council for the Arts, and the Ontario Arts Council
for their support of our publishing program. We acknowledge
the financial support of the Government of Canada through
the Canada Book Fund (CBF) for our publishing activities.

Cover and interior design by Tanya Montini
Cover image © Fancy Images / www.fotosearch.com
Printed in Canada by Friesens

Driftwood

Valerie Sherrard

FITZHENRY & WHITESIDE

For Christie Harkin
with gratitude and affection

Billy Lafferty stood at my front door with his hands shoved into the pockets of his saggy jeans. His shoulders slumped forward and his round, red face was glum. You never have to guess what kind of mood Billy is in.

"I can't go," he said.

It took me a few seconds to get what he was telling me. And that still didn't stop me from asking, "What do you *mean*, you can't go?"

"To the cottage. With you guys. My mom changed her mind." Billy scuffed his shoe against the worn cement on the step.

"But she said you could."

Billy shrugged. "Yeah, but now she says I can't."

"She can't change her mind like that," I said.

"Why not?"

"'Cause it's not fair."

Another shrug. Billy isn't much of a fighter. But this was way too important for him to just give up that way.

We'd been planning this for months, ever since April, when my dad told me that our family was going to do something different on our summer holidays. Most years, we spend a couple of weeks visiting relatives in Bobcaygeon, Ontario. So Dad's announcement was quite a surprise.

"This year, we're going to vacation right here in New Brunswick," Dad told me. "And not just for a few weeks, either. For the whole summer!"

"I need a change," Mom explained. "Lately, I haven't been able to paint. An artist's spirit needs room to breathe and grow."

"Your mother's work is important," Dad said. He tells me that a lot.

My mom paints the bridge. The covered bridge, that is. We live in Hartland, home of the world's longest covered bridge. People come from all over to see it, and lots of them buy my mom's paintings. The bridge in the summer, winter, spring, and fall. At sunrise, sunset, daylight, or under the pale glow of the moon. Whatever scene or season you want, my mom will have it.

"I've always been able to capture the *life* of the bridge," Mom said. "Everyone says so—you two know that. But not lately. It's become nothing but a structure. People aren't going to pay for that. If that's all they want, they can take a picture."

None of that mattered to me. I waited impatiently for Dad to tell me more about our plans.

Finally, he got to the point. "So, we're renting a cottage for two whole months!"

"A cottage? Where?"

Dad typed some words on his laptop and showed me where it was on a map of the province. "We'll be going to Miramichi, to a place called Schooner Point. Do you know what a schooner is, Adam?"

"A boat?"

"Not just any boat!" he said. There was a pause, then he turned to my mom.

"June, that's a schooner on our dime, isn't it?"

"It's the Bluenose," she answered.

"I know it's the Bluenose," he said. "Everyone knows that."

He turned back to me. "Now, I'm no expert on boats, son, but I do believe the Bluenose was a schooner. In fact, you can make a little project out of that this summer, while we're at the cottage. Find out all about schooners."

"Okay," I said. I knew it would be long forgotten before we ever got there. Dad gives me 'projects' all the time and then never thinks of them again. That suits me just fine.

"Oh, and there's one more thing," Dad said. "About our vacation, that is. Do you want to tell him, June, or will I?"

Mom smiled and said, "You go ahead, dear."

"Your mother and I talked it over and we decided

that you can invite a friend to come with you."

Now *that* was what I called awesome news. I was happy enough about going to a cottage, but taking a friend with me would make it perfect. Billy was my first, and really my only pick, and when he asked his mom she said he could come—though not for the whole summer. Dad promised to take him home partway through, and it was all set.

Until, that is, Billy, landed on my step the day before we were leaving, to say he couldn't come after all.

"Maybe my mom can talk your mom back into it," I said.

"Nope," Billy said gloomily. "Her mind's made up. Might as well not even get your mom to try. It'll just get my mom mad."

My mother took the news as a personal insult. "What does she think we're going to do, put Billy on a raft and set him adrift?" she grumbled to my dad.

"Less work for you, anyway," Dad said.

"I don't see how you figure that. What on earth is Adam going to do with himself without a friend along? He'll be under my feet all day." She glanced at me, sitting at the table. "You know what I mean, Adam. I'm just worried that you'll be bored."

"I was counting on Billy coming," I said. "I don't know why his mom's so mean."

"Well, I'm going to go ahead and give her a

call. What harm can it do?"

I hung around to see if I could tell from Mom's side of the conversation whether or not Billy's mom might budge. It didn't take long before I realized something was wrong. Mom confirmed it when she got off the phone.

"Mrs. Lafferty didn't say Billy couldn't go," she told me. "It was *his* decision."

I took off out the door and ran all the way to Billy's house. He was sitting under a big oak tree in their front yard. His mutt Bailey was lying beside him.

Billy saw me coming and he didn't look one bit happy about it.

"What's the big idea?" I said, tearing into his yard.

"Bailey's sick," he said without looking at me. "I can't leave him."

"That dog is always sick. He gets better every time!"

"Yeah, but the vet said this could be serious."

I'd heard that one a few times before, and said so to Billy. Bailey lifted his head a couple of inches and gave me a mournful look, but I knew his tricks. In a day or two, he'd be running around like nothing had ever been wrong with him.

"Anyway, your mom can take care of him," I said.

"He needs *me*. No one else takes care of him the way he likes."

I argued with him until it was plain he wasn't

going to budge. Looking at him sitting there with that dumb hound of his made me madder than I've ever been.

"I should have asked someone else," I yelled. "Someone who isn't a big fat liar like you."

"I didn't *want* to lie, I *had* to," Billy claimed. "'Cause you always get so mad."

"Why *wouldn't* I get mad for a dirty trick like this?"

"I'm not *trying* to do a dirty trick," Billy said. His face was as red as a fire truck. "I just can't leave Bailey. Not when he's so sick."

I stood there glowering while Billy hunched forward and stared at the grass. After a minute he lifted his head and said, "Maybe I can come after Bailey gets better."

"No. You can't. You can't come then and you can't come ever. You know why? 'Cause you ruin everything. I know I've told you this before, but this time I mean it a hundred percent. I am done being your friend."

I let that sink in and, just to make sure he got the message, I added, "Done, Billy. And I won't be changing my mind—not after this."

Billy shrugged like he didn't care, but I could see from the way his mouth was working that he was practically crying.

I didn't feel like seeing that, so I turned around and went home.

The drive to Schooner Point took about three and a half hours, which gave me plenty of time to think about how Billy had betrayed me. Over a dog. A scruffy, smelly dog, with a bunch of gunk around his eyes.

When we finally got there, I saw that our rental was an actual log cabin, one of a group of ten. We were assigned number 10. It was at the back corner of the cluster of buildings, and it was the coolest place I'd ever seen. My mom called it rustic, and said that it was just the right sort of place for the artist in her to come back to life.

"That's the spirit," Dad said. "Those old creative juices will be flowing in no time." Mom frowned a bit, but mostly she was looking around. So was I.

There are woods in behind the cabins, and a huge lake across the road. After the long drive, my feet were ready to take off and really check the place out. I was about to head to the shore when Dad stopped me.

"Adam, you can carry in anything that's not too heavy," he said.

Unloading the car took a while, mostly because Mom had a system. We had to sort everything according to some code she had marked on the boxes. Since she made up the codes, we had to ask about every single thing we brought in. Half the time she couldn't remember right away and then she stood there talking to herself until it came to her.

"You couldn't just label them with room names like anyone else?" Dad asked at one point.

Mom rolled her eyes. "You wouldn't understand, Doug," she said. "Creative people see things differently."

We were about halfway through the task of unloading when a woman appeared at the door. She rapped on the doorframe and stepped inside before anyone could say a word.

"Hi folks! Welcome to this little spot of heaven. I'm Monica Stillwater. Looks like we'll be neighbours for the next few weeks. This your first time here? Third time for me and my husband, Keith, and I can tell you, you're going to love it."

Dad smiled and reached his hand out to shake our visitor's. "Nice to meet you, Monica," he said. "We're Doug and June Orser and this is our son Adam."

Mom smiled too, but only a little. "I'm afraid you've caught us in the middle of getting settled in."

"No problem," Monica said. "I'll let you get back to it. Just wanted to be neighbourly and say hello. You be sure to drop over once you're unpacked and we can all get acquainted. We're two cabins down on your left."

Mom gave another small smile.

"Well, now, there's a friendly woman," Dad said after Monica had left. "Maybe you two will hit it off."

"She seems a bit pushy, if you ask me," Mom said. She peered at the box I'd just brought from the trunk. "DWCL," she read from the label. "Hmm. Just give me a minute and I'll tell you where that goes."

"Well, Adam, the roof rack is all unloaded and there's not that much in the trunk," Dad said, coming in with a suitcase a minute later. "I can handle it from here if you want to take a look around."

"Don't go far, though," Mom said. "And stay away from the water."

"I *know*, Mom," I said, hurrying out the door. She must have lectured me about not going in the water by myself about a million times before we even left home.

Outside, I made my way past a cluster of trees between the cabin and a dirt road that separated the cabins from the water. I crossed over and stood along the top of the bank, surprised at how wide open the water seemed. It was grey and cold-looking and straight ahead there was a place where it stretched on and on with no land in sight.

Something else that was different from what I'd imagined was the shore. It looked nothing like what I'd pictured. Instead of a wide, sandy beach, there was a stretch of wet sand and stones. The bank leading down to the water was covered with big, grey rocks.

As soon as I was sure I couldn't be seen from our cabin, I tugged off my shoes and put them on the ground. Then I made my way down across the rocks to the water's edge. I wasn't going in or anything, I just wanted to test the water and walk on the sand without shoes.

I was wiggling my toes in the water when something came flying through the air and landed near me with a big splash. My mouth dropped open when I saw that it was one of my shoes. I stared at it as it bobbed for a second and then sank out of sight.

My brain hardly had time to take this in before a voice called out from behind me.

"What's the big idea, leaving your stinky old shoes around to smell up the place?"

I turned and saw a kid around my age standing halfway down the bank. He was holding up the other shoe, and before I could say anything, it followed the first one through the air and into the water.

"Hey!" I said. At that, the kid turned and ran back up over the bank and out of sight.

I rolled my jeans up to the knee and waded slowly out to where the first shoe had landed. The waves were lapping close to my rolled-up pants, but I was pretty sure I could stay dry if I was careful. I got the first shoe and was almost to the second one when something swam by and brushed against my ankle. Of course, it didn't actually scare me but I jumped a bit because I hadn't been expecting it. My right foot came down on a slippery-smooth stone and shot out from under me. I grabbed at the air, which didn't help at all.

The next splash I heard was my butt hitting the water! I scrambled back to my feet as fast as I could, grabbed the other shoe, and made my way back to the shore.

Plunking down on a large rock, I dumped water out of the shoes and put them on the ground beside me. I wondered how long they would take to dry. Not that it really mattered. My clothes were soaked and I was going to have to explain how I got wet to my mom.

A movement behind me caught my attention while I was thinking this through. When I turned, I saw a face peeking at me from between two trees. It was the kid who'd thrown my shoes in the water.

"Hi," he said.

I didn't answer as I swivelled my head back to face the water again. But, besides being a jerk who throws people's shoes in the river, it seemed like he couldn't take a hint. He came closer, taking a step forward and pausing—I suppose to see if I was going to go after him. He probably figured he had a good chance to outrun me if I did. After all, he was wearing shoes.

I ignored him right until he sat down a couple of feet away.

"You're wet," he said.

I glared at him.

"I guess you fell in the water, huh?" he said.

"Thanks to *you*," I snapped. "Why'd you throw my shoes in?"

"I dunno." He hung his head down, like he was sorry, though I doubted it. "My mom said I had to go talk to you."

"So you threw my shoes in the water?"

"Yeah." He shook his head like he couldn't quite figure it out. He wasn't the only one.

"Well, now I'm going to get in trouble, and I might get grounded to the cabin or something," I said.

"Just on account of you're wet?"

"My mom doesn't want me in the water by myself," I told him, even though it was embarrassing to admit. "She's going to freak out."

"Maybe you could dry off before you go back. Then she won't know."

I leaned over and squeezed the rolled-up part of my jeans. Water dribbled down through my fingers. "They're soaking wet," I said. "They'll take forever to dry."

"My sister dries things really fast sometimes," he said. "We could ask her what to do."

I didn't see what it could hurt, so I shrugged, stood up and followed him across the road, through a cluster of trees and across the grassy lawn to his cabin. Number three.

"My name is Joey," he said, as we reached the door.

"I'm Adam," I told him.

"Sorry I threw your shoes in the water."

"It's okay."

We went in. Joey's mother made this big fuss that he'd "found himself a little friend." Poor guy. No wonder he went around throwing strangers' shoes in the river.

"Where's Lisa?" he asked when she'd stopped gushing.

"In her room, on the phone with Jean-Guy, as usual," his mom answered.

Joey headed toward a closed door, knocked and yelled that he was coming in. A girl's voice yelled back that he'd better not but a few seconds later the door swung open.

Lisa looked about sixteen. She was real pretty, even though she was frowning as she said, "What do *you* want?"

"Adam needs his clothes dried," Joey said. He

jerked a thumb backwards toward me.

Lisa's pink mouth went into some strange shapes while she stood there trying to figure out what Joey was talking about. She could see that my clothes were wet, which must have helped the message get through.

"Take 'em off," she said to me.

I stared in horror, which made her laugh.

"What's the matter? You all shy or something?" When I didn't answer, she laughed again and then said, "Oh, for goodness sakes! Just go put on something of Joey's for a few minutes."

I did as I was told and brought the soaked jeans and shirt back to her. By then, she had a big bath towel laid out flat on the floor. She wrung my clothes out by hand over the sink and then spread them on the towel, folded it in half, and rolled it up lengthwise. After that, she walked back and forth on top of it a couple of times.

"This good enough?" she asked, passing them back to me, "or do you need 'em completely dry right now? You can blow-dry them with my hair dryer if you want, but it'll take a while. It would be faster if you just put them back on and went outside. They'll dry in the air in no time now that most of the water is out."

I told her, "Thanks a lot." Sort of. The words that actually came out were kind of muffled and croaky. Lisa tousled my hair and laughed and told us to get lost.

I changed back into the cold, damp clothes, and Joey and I went outside so they could air dry like Lisa had said.

We sat on a picnic table near the cabin.

"How long are you guys staying here?" I asked him.

"Two weeks. We come here for the first half of July every summer," he said. After a minute, he added, "Lisa has a boyfriend."

"Shut up," I told him.

It wasn't long before I looked up to see my dad coming toward us. Luckily, I was pretty well dry, except for my shoes.

"Howdy there, stranger," he said, nodding at Joey and sticking out his hand when he reached us.

"Uh, howdy," Joey said. He shook Dad's hand but he didn't look too excited about it.

"Sorry to break up this party, partner, but we've gotta go rustle up some grub," Dad told me.

"Does Adam have to go?" Joey asked. "'Cause my mom wouldn't mind watching him."

Dad hesitated, looking over his shoulder toward our cabin. He seemed to be thinking about it, which Joey saw as a chance to race the few steps to his cabin door and get his mom. She came outside and told Dad she'd be more than happy to keep an eye on me for a while. That settled it and a few minutes later Mom and Dad drove off, waving like they weren't going to see me for months.

"Your dad talks kinda weird," Joey observed.

"He always does that for the first few days when we go on vacation," I said. "I don't know why."

"Doesn't it embarrass you?" Joey asked.

"Well, sure, but what can I do about it?"

"That's true," he said. His head snapped up with a thought. "Hey, you want to make some money?"

"Okay," I said. "How?"

"There's an old guy who lives up that way," Joey said, with a vague wave, "and he pays for hunks of driftwood that wash up on shore."

"How come?"

"I dunno. He makes stuff out of them or something and he can't find any himself because he's blind."

I wasn't all that keen, but there was nothing else to do so I shrugged and said, "Okay then."

"He pays five bucks if it's good enough for him to use. Come on, I'll show you where he lives, and we can check the shore on the way."

I followed him across the road and down to the water's edge. I noticed that he ignored the road for taking boats to the water, just like I had earlier. It's way better to climb down over a bunch of rocks.

We kept our eyes peeled for pieces of driftwood as we made our way along the curve of the shore line.

It was a fairly long walk and for awhile there was nothing promising. The wet sand was covered in stones, some shells, and a few scruffy twigs that nobody could possibly want. Then I noticed a branch partly buried in the sand where the curve of the bank began. I hurried over and tugged it free. It wasn't very big, but I thought it looked kind of interesting.

"Are you nuts or what?" Joey shouted when he saw what I had. "He's not gonna want that scraggly thing."

He was probably right, but I held onto it anyway while Joey had himself a good laugh. When he finally quieted down a bit I said, "I'll be the one laughing if it gets me five bucks."

"No fear of that," he snickered.

"You never know."

Joey shook his head but he quit laughing and he didn't say anything else for a couple of minutes. I could tell I'd gotten to him when he said, "No way Theo will want that. But, suppose he did— we'd be splitting the money, right?"

"Wrong," I said. "I found this and all you did was make fun of it."

"Yeah, but I told you about him and everything. We'd have to be partners. It's only fair."

"No way," I said.

"Then maybe I won't even take you there."

I didn't answer him and, though he scowled at me a couple of times, he didn't make good on his threat. We kept walking, and before long he pointed up the bank.

"There it is. That's where he lives."

I don't think I would have seen the house at all, if he hadn't shown it to me. It was a tiny place tucked away in the woods that sprouted up past the crest of the bank. The outside of the house had grey shingles that blended in with the tree trunks and the roof was covered in some kind of moss.

Joey and I scrambled up the bank and snaked our way in among the trees until we were standing in the small clearing that surrounded the house. And there, sitting outside on a faded back deck, was an old man in a wooden rocking chair.

"Hello! Hello!" he said. "Who's there?"

"It's me—Joey," Joey said, "And I brought someone with me—Adam. He's staying in one of the cabins too."

"Pleased to make your acquaintance, young man," the old guy said. He looked in my direction but not right at me. "My name is Theo Banyan."

"Hi," I said. It felt like that wasn't enough— like I should say something else, so I added, "I'm Adam, sir," even though Joey had already told him my name.

"Call me Theo," he said. "Everyone does."

"Yes, sir—I mean, Theo."

We were close enough now that I could see the old man's eyes. They were strange looking—

like someone had painted white clouds over the coloured parts.

The old man nodded and smiled and said, "Someone has taught you good manners."

"Yes, sir, Theo," I said. "It was my mom. She doesn't want our relations to think I was raised in a barn."

"Good manners are like keys," he said. "Did you know that?"

I wondered if this was some sort of a puzzle, or if maybe Theo was a little odd.

"Keys? Like for doors?" Joey asked.

"For doors, yes. And for other things too—like treasures and trophies and an old man's heart."

I had no idea what that meant, and by the look on Joey's face, neither did he. He shrugged a shoulder at me and then turned back to our host.

"Say, Theo," Joey said, "Adam is going to be here for the whole summer."

"Is that so?" Theo said. I noticed that his hands were resting on his knees. Veins stuck up on the backs of them like really skinny worms. His fingers were long and boney.

"His parents went to buy food," Joey continued. "Or 'grub,' as his dad called it."

"Speaking of grub," Theo said with a chuckle, "would either of you boys care for an oat cake?"

"Not me," said Joey.

"I never heard of an oat cake before," I said. I

thought that might sound rude so I added, "But I bet it's real good."

"Well, you just wait right here and I'll bring one out so you can try it," Theo said. He stood up slowly, moving his arms and legs like he was testing to make sure everything worked. Then he took a few careful steps to the cabin door and disappeared inside.

"You'll be sorry," Joey told me as soon as Theo was out of sight.

"What do you mean?"

"You think you're getting a delicious hunk of *cake*, don't you? Well, you're *not*. It's going to be a hard old cookie. You just watch."

I looked nervously at the doorway and saw Theo on his way back. He was holding a small plate with a flat, pale cookie on it.

"Adam?" he said once he was on the veranda again.

I stepped closer. "I'm here," I said. The cookie didn't look any better up close.

"Here's your oat cake," Theo said. He sounded proud and pleased. I reached out and took it. It felt hard all right and dry, but I said thanks anyway.

"Enjoy!" Theo said with a smile.

"It looks great," I lied. I lifted it slowly toward my face but it was like my mouth didn't want to open. It took some effort but I forced myself to nibble a tiny bit off the edge. It wasn't delicious, but, honestly, it wasn't that bad either. Mostly, it was kind of bland but I could taste the oatmeal in it, and I like oatmeal okay.

I was about to tell Theo that it was good when an odd look came over his face. His hand reached down, sweeping the air on my left side. When it connected with the piece of driftwood I'd found on the shore, his head popped up and his smile got even wider.

"Is this for me, Adam?" he asked, taking hold of it.

I nodded. Then I realized he couldn't see that so I said, "Yes. I picked it up on the way here."

"I *told* him it was no good, but you know Adam. He brought it anyway," Joey said with a snort. "Don't worry, I already explained how you only pay for the ones you want."

My mouth flapped a couple of times while my face turned red. I was madder than I'd been when Joey threw my shoes in the water. Then Theo spoke up, and what he said kind of calmed me down.

"Well, I certainly want *this* one." His voice quivered in excitement as his hands ran up and down the branch. "It's a beauty."

Joey's face was something to see. I wished I could have got a picture of it to show him later.

Theo sat himself back into his chair and held that piece of wood. He got quiet for a minute, in a way that made me and Joey quiet too. Theo stroked the wood gently and his fingers kind of vibrated on it, like it was too cold to touch.

"This is a wonderful, wonderful piece of driftwood," he said after a moment. "Would you boys like to know where it came from?"

"Where it came from?" I echoed. "How can you tell that?"

"I can tell," Theo said simply. He got a look on his face like he was seeing something a long way off and when he began to speak, his voice seemed faraway too, and somehow strange. It was as if the words he spoke were coming from someone else. Someone from another time and place.

THE LYCHEE

This piece of driftwood is from a lychee tree. It has seen hundreds of seasons and weathered many storms. It has crossed wide oceans and passed endless miles of shore on its travels to this place.

Life began for this tree several centuries ago, in a tiny village on the eastern coast of China. In this village lived a man named Suen Qiu.

Suen Qiu was not a remarkable man. He lived a quiet life, working in his orchard, playing with his children, and talking to his wife and her parents, for they all shared one home. Suen Qiu ate when he was hungry and slept when he was tired. He found pleasure in simple things, such as listening to his wife sing of the Jasmine flower, or eating a steaming bowl of geng.

In the village where Suen Qiu and his family lived, almost everyone made their living in the same way—as lychee farmers. Everywhere you looked, your eyes would find row upon row of lychee trees in the great orchards that surrounded the village.

Perhaps you have never seen this kind of fruit. Let me tell you a little bit about it. The lychee tree grows about as tall as an apple tree. Its long, pointed leaves are the beautiful colour of a fine emerald. The lychee fruit has an outer shell, usually a shade of red, and while it is about the size of a small plum it looks more like a raspberry. Once you peel off the red outer layer, there is a delicious white globe inside with a seed buried right in the centre.

The people of Suen Qiu's village worked very hard caring for their lychee groves, planting and pruning and protecting. In the fall they would harvest the lychees and sell them to a middleman who then took the fruit to cities and sold it to merchants. Year after year, everything went along just as it should. And then came the summer of the great crop failure.

The first sign of trouble came when it was time for the lychee trees to bloom. Some trees put out breathtaking blooms, and people love them for their beauty. This is not true of the lychee tree. Few people would find its blossoms pretty. To the lychee farmer's eyes, however, they are a beautiful sight, for they mean that the lychee will soon follow.

In the year of the great crop failure, this did not happen. The blossoms seemed to be forming, but then they shrivelled and died away. The village was soon abuzz with the sound of people discussing the matter. What could have happened? Was it possible the trees would make another attempt at blooming?

They watched and waited, Suen Qiu among them. Nothing happened. The trees did not bloom again, although they looked healthy in all other ways. Fear crept over the villagers. What would happen to them? How would they provide for their families in the coming year if they did not have any lychees to sell to the middleman at harvest time? They worried and fretted but this did not make any difference to their circumstances.

Suen Qiu looked at his family and his heart was heavy. His wife no longer smiled or sang the song of the Jasmine flower as she went about her work. Her lips were pressed closed so the song could not get out. Suen Qiu's mother-in-law and father in-law looked at him with anger, as though he had somehow brought this misfortune to them. Only his children were unchanged. They played and studied and did their chores as always because they trusted that their father would take care of them. Suen Qiu felt this was the greatest burden of all for he could see that he would soon fail even in his children's eyes.

One day, Suen Qiu walked through his orchard, asking himself questions. What can I do? What will become of my family? But these were not questions he could answer and so there was great unrest in his mind.

And then, near the end of one row, Suen Qiu made a discovery. On the far side of one of his lychee trees was a single blossom. This was unusual as the lychee always blossoms in clusters.

In a rush of anger, Suen Qiu's hand reached toward it. What value was a single lychee blossom? No fruit would grow without both the male and female flower, each doing their part. And even if it was somehow pollinated, what good would it be? One lychee from an entire grove! It was as if the lone flower had grown there just to mock him. Suen Qiu would tear this blossom from the tree and fling it to the ground.

But before he could carry out this plan, Suen Qiu stopped. He asked himself why he should punish this flower, which was a living thing. It had not done anything to harm him. And so he left it and continued on his walk.

Many pressing matters occupied Suen Qiu's mind and it was several days before he thought of the blossom again. He decided to check on it, even though he felt sure that it would be gone.

But it was not gone. In fact, the flower had given way to a tiny lychee, young and green. Suen Qiu stood there looking at it for some time.

He did not know if it made him feel better or worse. When he returned to his home, he did not mention the lychee to anyone.

As the days passed, Suen Qiu listened carefully to the talk in the village. He wondered if any of the other farmers might have made similar discoveries but it soon became clear he was the only one. Even so, he told no one of his lychee.

The next week, Suen Qiu went back to see how the lychee was doing. He was surprised to see that it had grown to the size of his fist. This was very strange—an impossible thing. It seemed that someone must be playing a trick on him. Suen Qiu examined the lychee carefully from all sides until he was satisfied that it was real.

From that day on, Suen Qiu visited the lychee faithfully. He spent hours sitting at the base of the tree, watching and wondering. It was his hope that he could come to understand what was happening, for the lychee was growing at an astonishing rate. Sometimes it seemed that it had almost doubled in size overnight. Suen Qiu felt a new hope stir in him, and yet that hope also made him afraid. Still, he told no one.

But Suen Qiu's wife had noticed that something was different about her husband. One afternoon she watched him go into the orchard and she decided to follow him. When she reached the tree and saw the lychee, which was now larger than a watermelon, she clapped her hand over her mouth and sank to her knees. She asked her husband what this meant. He could not tell her.

The next day, two more were added to those who knew of the secret lychee when Suen Qiu's wife told her parents. They hurried to the tree to see with their own eyes, for their daughter's words had not convinced them.

Each day that passed, the lychee continued to grow. It grew so large that the tree bent under its weight. Suen Qiu and his father-in-law built a wooden brace to help support its weight. As they worked, the older man asked Suen Qiu what he meant to do with the lychee.

"I have given this much thought," Suen Qiu answered. "When the lychee is ripe I hope to sell it for a great price—enough money to divide among all the villagers."

"That is a good plan," said the old man. "There is even a small chance that you will have enough money to care for your own family if you do this. My only worry is that some of the villagers will feel you have insulted them. Not everyone takes kindly to a handout."

Suen Qiu had not thought of that. He did not want the villagers to think he was proud, or that he viewed himself as some kind of hero. It was strange to think that he would be judged for helping others but he did not believe he had a choice. Surely it was the right thing to do.

When the lychee started to turn red and its

prickly bumps began to grow smooth, Suen Qiu's father-in-law asked him once again what he meant to do. He smiled when Suen Qiu told him his plan was unchanged and that he still meant to share whatever money the lychee brought with everyone in the village.

"That is because you have a good heart," said the older man. He nodded and appeared to be thinking hard. "And yet, I wonder—"

"What?" asked Suen Qiu. "What do you wonder?"

"I cannot help but think that your actions will insult the Fates that brought this good fortune to you. It would be very wrong to defy fate when it is clear you have been chosen. Perhaps you are meant to use this lychee to gain a position of power so that you can help many, rather than just these few villagers."

Suen Qiu had not thought of this possibility. He no longer knew what he should do. His thoughts raced in a terrible circle and he knew no peace. They stole his sleep and created great turmoil in his mind.

Each day, as he walked in the orchard and stood by the lychee, Suen Qiu hoped for a sign. If only there was some way to know for certain what he should do, he would gladly do that thing.

The days passed by, one by one, as Suen Qiu struggled with his thoughts. And then, one morning when he went to the tree, a terrible sight met his eyes. The lychee, which had been fully ripe for several days, had broken the wooden brace. The branch that held it was torn from the tree and the great fruit lay on the ground, split wide open. Worst of all, small animals and bugs had found it and feasted on it all through the night. There was nothing left that could be salvaged, nothing of any value.

Suen Qiu wept.

"Well, what happened after that?" Joey blurted when Theo had been silent for a moment.

"That's all I know," Theo said. He held up the piece of driftwood and added, "But *this* is the very branch that held the great lychee."

Then Theo gave me five dollars for bringing the driftwood and told us he needed a rest but we were welcome to come see him again any time. He said I should bring my mom and dad to meet him soon, too.

On our walk back to the cabins I thought Joey would ask for half of the money, but when he spoke it was only to say, "You think that story was true?"

"It sure *sounded* true," I said.

"I wonder what happened to Suen Qiu after the lychee busted open."

"I dunno."

"What do you think he should have done with it?" Joey said.

"He should have shared. For sure."

Neither of us said anything else the rest of the way back to the cabins. When we got there, I stopped at the canteen for change and gave Joey half of the five dollars.

I was at the table having breakfast with Mom and Dad a few mornings later when a knock came at our door. I ran to open it, thinking it would be Joey, as usual, but it was the woman who'd come to welcome us the day we first got there.

"Good morning!" she said. "It's me, Monica Stillwater—in case you've forgotten. I stopped by for a minute the other day? Anyway, I thought I'd pop over and bring you some muffins, fresh out of the oven."

"They smell great!" Dad said, crossing the room to the door. He took the paper plate of muffins she was holding and held them up for a closer sniff. "Mmm, hmm. I can tell already that they're delicious. Can you smell these over there, June?"

"Yes," Mom said. "They do smell good."

"They're my own recipe—apple spice muffins," Monica told us. "I get a lot of compliments on them—not to toot my own horn." She giggled at that and then kind of stood there.

"Would you like to come in and have a cup of coffee with us? While we dig into these wonderful muffins?" my dad asked.

Mom looked startled and not too happy, but she pushed those things off her face and smiled as Monica hurried over to the table.

"Are you sure I'm not imposing?" Monica asked as she nestled herself onto a chair. "I surely didn't meant to intrude—why, it looks like you're right in the middle of your breakfast!"

"It's fine," Mom said. "Anyway, I'll be setting up my easel and painting later, so this is really the only time I'd have for a visit today."

"You're an *artist*?" Monica's eyes got rounder. "I've always wanted to paint, you know? I even signed up for lessons once, but then other things came up so I couldn't go."

Mom didn't say anything to that but I could tell she was annoyed. She doesn't like it when people talk as if anyone at all can paint. She says if you're not born with the gift, you're not a *true* artist.

"So, you and your husband come here every summer," Dad said. "Is it just the two of you?"

"Yep. Just me and Keith," Monica said. "He spends his days on the water but I like my feet on solid ground, if you know what I mean. Say, maybe you and the little guy here would like to go out in the boat with Keith sometime."

Dad said that would be great and I could tell he

meant it. I thought so, too, but Joey came along just then so I didn't find out if it was actually going to happen. Sometimes people say we should do this or that when they don't really mean it. Or, if they *do* mean it, they must forget because they never do it.

I'd hardly made it down our cabin steps when Mom appeared in the doorway. It seemed she had to say the same thing every time I went out the door.

"Remember, you can go to the shore but stay out of the water."

"Don't worry, we're going in the woods today!" Joey announced, like it was all decided.

"Well, don't go too far," Mom said. "Make sure you can still see the cabins or other houses from wherever you are."

We said we would and Mom disappeared back into the cabin. The second she did, Joey grabbed my arm and gave me a tug. "Come on," he said in a loud whisper. "Let's get outta here before your mom starts worrying about bears and wolves."

I ran with him and we darted into the woods. I noticed that the trees were bare a long ways up, which made me wonder out loud why there were no leaves on the lower part.

"There's a spell on them that only lets them grow leaves at the top," Joey said, looking around and up. "That's because this forest is home to the moss people."

"No, it's not," I said.

"How do you know?"

"There's no such thing," I answered.

"Yeah? Well, I guess you didn't see the strange-looking animals in that big open field on the way in here."

That got my attention all right. I knew exactly what he was talking about. We'd seen what looked like a shrunken donkey and some kind of creature with a bizarre hump on its shoulder among an assortment of goats and cows. I'd asked Dad about the one with the hump but I don't think he knew. He said finding out could be a great summer project for me.

I looked around nervously.

"It's safe in here most of the time," Joey said. "Unless you do something the moss people don't like. If you get the moss people mad, they put one of their spells on you."

"Oh, sure," I said. I made a kind of laughing sound. "And what do their spells do?"

"One spell makes you grow big, ugly lumps on you, like some of those animals in the field. You can tell which ones bothered the moss people just by looking at them. But that's not the worst spell. The worst spell turns *you* into a moss person."

Of course, I didn't believe moss people existed. I'm not gullible that way, not like my EX-friend Billy would have been. After we'd been tromping around for a while, I forgot all about them.

Until, suddenly, Joey disappeared.

The first thing I did was call his name a few times. I stood very still, listening carefully. I could hear lots of woods sounds, rustling and crackling and snapping and such, but there was no answer from Joey.

"I know you're hiding, Joey!" I said, good and loud. My voice wasn't quite as steady as I wanted it to be.

Suddenly, all the noises in the forest seemed to be creeping closer. I felt something prickle against my neck, which made me jump. I might have kind of yelped a bit too. I turned slowly, looking all around me. If Joey was somewhere nearby, I sure didn't see him.

Ka-THUMP, Ka-THUMP, Ka-THUMP. That's how loud I could hear my heart pounding in my ears. And then I realized the worst thing of all. I didn't know the way back. We'd lost sight of the cabins a while ago but I hadn't worried about it. Joey had seemed to know where he was going.

But now, Joey was gone and I was lost and some of the sounds around me didn't seem so harmless anymore. Not too far away a branch snapped, as though it had been stepped on.

Someone—*or something*—was coming. I wasn't thinking about moss people or anything dumb like that. Not seriously. But I remembered that Joey had mentioned bears and wolves when we first started out.

What if this wasn't a joke? What if something had gotten him, and now it was after me, too? I called his name again.

No answer. Another snap. Then another.

"Joey, if that's you, this isn't funny."

The next sound was more like a thump. That's when I knew for sure.

Something was coming—and it was coming to get me.

My legs were trembling but somehow I forced them to move and once they got going they worked all right. I ran and ran, crashing through the ferns and bushes, darting around trees, racing away from whatever dark, terrible thing was after me. I ran until my legs turned rubbery and my chest felt like it was going to burst.

When I stopped it was more to catch my breath than anything else. I dropped to my knees, gulping air. That was when I found out I hadn't been fast enough.

Fingers of moss were touching my face. I felt them reaching for my throat.

The moss people were real!

My hands jerked up, ready to fight back even though I knew it was probably hopeless. I clawed desperately at the fingers clutching my throat and, to my surprise, they let go. Not only did they let go—I saw that I was holding long, frail moss fingers in my hands. They hung there—limp, green strands that didn't seem to be attached to anything.

It took a minute for my brain to figure out what was going on. Once it did, I would have laughed except it was embarrassing to think about how terrified I'd been.

The "fingers" that had been about to choke me weren't fingers at all. They were thin, loose wisps of some kind of dry moss. Now that I'd calmed myself, I saw that it was drooping down from a big cluster growing on the side of a tree.

I felt pretty foolish, even though nobody had

seen me. Then I got mad at Joey. It was his dumb story about moss people that had started everything. Plus there was that disappearing act he pulled. I bet he was watching the whole time I was calling for him. Now, he was probably somewhere killing himself laughing about the way I'd bolted.

That made me wonder again where he'd gone. I decided I didn't care. I'd find my way back to the cabins by myself. That would teach him.

And then I had a better idea. I hauled down big hunks of the moss and got busy. In a few minutes there was moss threaded in my hair, hanging down across my face, coming out my ears and sticking out the sleeves of my t-shirt and shorts. I rubbed some dirt on my face and arms too. A few minutes later, as I moved carefully through the woods, I saw some red berries. I squeezed a few and dabbed the red juice on my neck and forehead and dribbled some from the corners of my mouth, down my chin. I sure would have liked to see how it all looked.

My mad dash through the woods had broken ferns and other plants, and my shoes had dug up clumps of soft earth and dried nettles. I decided to follow the trail I'd made, retracing my steps—first to the last place I'd seen Joey, and then back toward the cabins. With any luck, I'd meet up with Joey.

It was probably ten minutes later when I heard Joey coming through the woods. He was calling,

"Adam," over and over, but not very loud. When you're alone, the woods can feel pretty scary and the sound of his voice told me he was getting more and more nervous.

I stopped walking and stood very, very still, looking hard for any sign of movement. I waited until I could just barely see him in the distance. Taking a couple of steps to the left made it easy for me to keep him in sight while I was hidden by bushes.

Then, I groaned, but I was careful not to do it too loud. That would make it too obvious. It would be better if Joey had to strain a bit to hear it.

He stopped moving. I could tell by the way he tipped his head a bit that he was listening. He called my name a couple more times. When there was no answer he started to move in my direction again. He was walking real slow, looking around, and I saw him wipe his forehead with the back of his hand a couple of times.

I waited until he was a stone's throw away and then I started making strained breathing sounds. Joey stopped moving again. I could see by his expression that he was trying hard to talk himself out of being terrified. He took a deep breath and inched a few steps closer but he was moving about as fast as a snail.

As soon as I figured he was close enough, I whispered, "*Heeeeelp meeee.*" Joey's eyes nearly bugged out.

It was time to move. I lumbered forward with my arms out a few inches from my sides. I made gurgling sounds and then rasped out another, "*Heeeelp meee, Jooo-eeey.*"

For a couple of seconds, Joey was frozen in place. His face turned mushroom-white and his eyes practically bulged out of his skull. A strangled sound came out of him and after a bit of effort it turned into the kind of scream a nine-year-old girl might let out if you dropped a snake down the back of her shirt.

I took another slow step toward him and that snapped him into action. He turned and started to run—except, in his panic, he ran smack into a tree. You'd have thought he was made of rubber the way he bounced off it and landed on the ground.

"*Please!*" he yelled. "Please, don't hurt me."

"Don't worry, I won't hurt you, Joey," I said. "And *you* should probably stop slamming yourself into trees."

I hardly got the words out when the laughter I'd been holding in came bursting out. I laughed so hard that I bent over at the waist and then ended up sinking to the ground. While I gasped for breath, I saw Joey pulling himself up and glaring at me. I figured he'd be mad but he surprised me by breaking into a grin.

"You got me good," he said, his smile growing. "I never woulda thought you had it in you."

"And I never woulda thought you could screech like a girl," I said.

Joey laughed at that. Then he tossed a handful of nettles at me and stood up, brushing himself off. "You look disgusting," he said admiringly.

"I wouldn't mind seeing it for myself," I told him, "but this moss is itching something awful." I started yanking it out of my clothes and hair.

"Even without the moss you look pretty gross," Joey said. "Is your mom going to freak out when she sees you?"

"I doubt it," I told him. "My mom mostly cares about safety stuff. She doesn't usually get mad at me for getting dirty."

Joey didn't look convinced. "Well, it's not just dirt," he said. "You look like you're bleeding, too."

I'd forgotten about the berries!

"Oh, yeah. Maybe I *should* clean up before I go home," I said.

"You can do it at my place," Joey offered.

We decided to head out of the woods. Joey said his throat was dryer than heck and he could go for a nice, cold drink of water. Hearing that made me realize that *my* throat was dryer than heck, too. After that, every minute that went by made me more and more thirsty.

Joey insisted he knew where to go at first but after a while he dropped the act and admitted he had no idea where we were. At least, that's how I took it when he said, "Let's hope we can make it back to civilization before the sun goes down."

"Are we lost? Honest?" I asked.

"Maybe a little, but not really," he said. "If we have to, one of us can climb a tree to see which way the water is."

I didn't worry much after that, and it turned out that we weren't too far from the cabins anyway. Once they were in sight, we stopped to figure out how to sneak past my cabin to get to Joey's. We crouched and skulked in around trees and cars without being spotted.

"We did it," Joey said, letting out a big breath once we'd dashed the last couple of yards into his cabin. "I thought for sure the enemy would have us in their sights, but we outsmarted them."

"The *enemy*?" came a voice from behind us.

We turned to see Lisa, sitting at the table, eating a sandwich. Her eyes widened when she saw me. Then, she shook her head and said, "Go wash your face, you're grossing me out."

She might be pretty but she sure knew how to take the fun out of things.

Monica Stillwater was driving my mom clean out of her mind. At least, that's what Mom told Dad as I was finishing my lunch one day.

"That woman cannot take a hint," Mom said. I couldn't see her face from where I was sitting, but the way her words were coming out told me her teeth were clamped together. I mostly see her do that when she's talking about tourists who don't know the first thing about art.

"They're only here for a few more days, June," Dad said. "Try not to let it get to you."

"Seriously, Doug? Don't let it get to me? She's been here practically *every morning* since we got here."

"I know, dear," Dad said. Of course he knew. How could he *not* know? He was right there with us at breakfast every day that Monica Stillwater knocked at the door. I don't think he really minded. Monica always brought something with her. Muffins, biscuits, cinnamon rolls, croissants, cornbread—it was never the same thing twice. Everything she made was delicious and Dad never stopped at one helping.

"She knows we have no choice but to ask her in," Mom said. "Not when she's standing there with her infernal baking. She's using baked goods to force herself on us!"

"At least it's only in the mornings," Dad said. And he was right, except for that very moment when a sound outside the door made us all turn to look.

And there was Monica Stillwater. Her face was about the colour of the berries I'd used for fake blood that day in the woods.

Dad took a few giant steps and pulled the door open. "Monica?" he said, like he wasn't quite sure.

Monica didn't look at any of us. Her voice sounded choked when she spoke.

"I just came by to ask if you and Adam were free tomorrow, Doug. Keith said it would be a good day for the two of you to go along with him on the boat."

"*Honest?*" I blurted, before I had time to think.

"Yes, honest." Monica gave me a sad smile. "Is nine o'clock all right?" she asked Dad.

"Yes, nine is fine," Dad said. "Great. But, I, uh, that is, I think I should explain—"

"No, please don't," Monica said. Then she hurried down the steps and away.

"How was I supposed to know she was there?" Mom said. She plunked herself into the wooden rocking chair and folded her arms in front of her. Her easel was in that corner and the canvas perched on it had the beginning of a painting that hadn't seen much progress in the time we'd been at Schooner Point. Mom glanced at it and started to cry.

I wasn't sure if she was crying about Monica, or the painting or both. I went over and patted her arm and said, "It's okay, Mom," but that just made her cry harder.

That made me think it was a good time to go for a walk. I was on my own that day since Joey and his family had gone on a day trip to Hopewell Rocks. It had been fun hanging out with Joey for the past week and a half—*way* more fun than it would have been with Billy—but now they were down to their last few days.

I headed down to the shore and ambled along for a while. I was looking for driftwood or anything else that might be interesting. All I found was a couple of dead jellyfish and I knew better than to touch them.

Mom was staring at her easel when I wandered back to the cabin later. There was a brush in her hand, but it hadn't been dipped in paint. Dad was at the table, tapping away on his laptop.

"How's it going there, Adam?" he asked.

"Okay, I guess. There's not much to do with Joey gone."

"You could go see Theo." He and Mom had met Theo our first week there and they liked him so much they'd brought him over for supper one night. He'd told us stories about when he was young. They were cool but nothing like the story of Suen Qiu and the lychee.

"He doesn't have time to go there right now," Mom said. "We're eating soon."

"It's okay," I said, "I'll just do something on my iPod for a while."

"That reminds me," Mom said, "There was an alert of some sort from Billy on that thing when you were out yesterday."

"Okay." I took the iPod to my room so she wouldn't know I was ignoring Billy. I hadn't told my folks I wasn't friends with him anymore. That would only lead to a bunch of questions and speeches.

When I checked my iPod I saw that he'd sent a message saying he hoped I wasn't still mad. I deleted it without answering.

⸺

"I hope this won't be awkward," Dad said as we crossed the road and walked through the field to the water. It was the next morning and we were on our way to join Keith Stillwater on his boat.

Dad had said the exact same thing while we were eating breakfast earlier. There'd been no fear of Monica showing up at the door this time—or ever again.

"Maybe she didn't mention anything to Keith," Mom said. "Don't you think he would have found an excuse to cancel if he knew?"

"Or, she told him and he's planning to toss me overboard," Dad said.

"Doug! Watch what you say in front of Adam!" Mom said.

I looked up from my cereal. "It's okay, Mom. I knew it was a joke."

"It will probably be fine," Dad said. "And you'll have some time all to yourself, like you've been wanting."

Mom looked over at the unchanged easel in the corner. She didn't say anything.

Dad and I finished eating, got ready and headed to the water. Keith was already there. He waved and greeted us like we'd been buddies for years.

"Should be a good day on the water," he said. "Sunny, with just enough breeze to keep us cool."

We all put on life jackets and in no time we were on the boat, heading away from shore. Everything about it was fantastic! The way the boat zipped along, the air rushing against my face, the smell of the water—I loved it all.

Keith steered the boat expertly. We travelled

up the Miramichi River and then Keith said we were going to circle Sheldrake Island and head out to the village of Escuminac. I kept looking off at where the water seemed to go on forever with no land in sight.

"Is that the ocean?" I asked.

"Now *that* would make a real interesting summer project for you," Dad said. "You could find out all about the bodies of water around here."

Keith gave Dad a funny look. Then he gestured in the direction I'd pointed. "Let me get you started on that," he said. "A fair way to the east of here, that wide open water becomes the Gulf of St. Lawrence. The North Atlantic Ocean is a fair number of miles beyond that."

Dad says you remember things better if you find them out for yourself. I don't know for sure if it counts when you find out by asking someone and I didn't want to forget what Keith had told me so I went over it in my head a few times.

It took a while for us to get to Escuminac. That was fine with me. Everything was perfect—the warm sun, the glittering water and the way the boat skittered along on the waves. Once we were there, we docked at a huge wharf. Keith said it was the largest inshore wharf in Canada.

We checked out a big monument there. It was about a storm in 1959, when thirty-five fishermen were lost at sea. After we looked that over, we bought some deep fried clams with French fries and coleslaw for lunch. Then, we went walking on the beach.

We were on our way back to the boat when I noticed a bit of wood sticking out of the warm, dry sand. I got to work, scooping and digging, but when I tugged the rest of it free, it turned out to be a flat old board. I would have left it there, only Keith looked it over and said he thought it might be a piece of plank, possibly from a ship. So, I brought it with me because you never know.

Joey had his usual laugh when I showed it to him the next day.

"Do you think maybe you got a little too much sun?" he asked, slapping the side of his leg.

"It might be from a ship," I said, like that was my own idea.

"More like it might be from a *barn*!" Joey howled with laughter. "But, come on! Let's take it to Theo. I can't wait to see this!"

Joey is the kind of guy who takes a long time to run out of smart-aleck things to say. By the time we got to Theo's place, I was wishing I'd left that wood on the beach where I found it.

Theo had hardly gotten himself into his chair on the porch when Joey announced that I'd made a great find.

"Wait 'til you get a load of this!" he said. He grabbed the chunk of wood from me and laid it in Theo's lap.

Theo took hold of it and ran his hands lightly

over the surface. His face grew serious as he stroked it and turned it over. When he opened his mouth, instead of speaking, he began to sing in a thin, warbling voice.

A life on the ocean wave!
A home on the rolling deep
Where the scattered waters rave,
And the winds their revels keep!

Joey and I gave each other a look. You probably know the kind I mean. And Theo, even though he couldn't see us, must have sensed something because he started to chuckle.

"I'll quit there for now," he said. "But if you have time, I'll tell you about this bit of wood, which has reached us from many decades in the past. And a most interesting past it was."

We told him we had plenty of time and after a moment, Theo began to speak.

THE OAK

About two hundred years ago, in a coastal town in northern Europe, a young man named Jozefat lived with his Aunt Katarzyna. She was a widow who had taken care of her nephew since his parents perished in a boating accident. Even though Jozefat's aunt was poor, she managed to stretch what little she had in order to provide for him.

Katarzyna had never had children of her own. She loved her nephew and treated him like a son. As Jozefat grew, she sacrificed more and more in order to give him as much as she could.

Katarzyna was poor, but she had one prized possession. That was a splendid oak tree that grew at the side of her humble dwelling. It was the most majestic oak that had ever been seen in those parts.

"When your uncle Piotr asked me to marry

him," she sometimes told Jozefat, "he said that he could promise me very little, but that if I would be his wife, he would build us a home in this very place, and we would always have this tree to shelter us. It is the only comfort left to me. Someday I will be buried under its branches and rest there forever beside my dear Piotr."

Jozefat thought this attachment to a tree was a trifle foolish. He especially thought so anytime a lumber broker offered a large sum of money if Katarzyna would let him cut down the massive oak and harvest its wood.

"Some things are not for sale," Katarzyna would say. And that would be that.

At such times, Jozefat could only shake his head. "Silly old woman," he would mutter under his breath. It was his plan to sell the tree as soon as his aunt was gone. "I'll plant another tree to shelter the graves," he told himself, when he remembered her burial wishes.

Then something happened that changed everything. Jozefat met a young woman named Halina and he fell in love with her. Halina loved him too, but her family would not agree to the marriage because Jozefat was so poor.

The young sweethearts despaired until Jozefat devised a plan. He would trick his aunt into going on a trip with him, and while they were away, he would have the great oak tree harvested. The money he would receive would be more than enough to convince Halina's parents that he was a good prospect for their daughter.

Deceiving the old woman proved easier than he could have hoped. Before long the two had set off on what Katarzyna believed was a holiday her nephew had arranged to please her. For those few weeks, her heart sang with joy. It seemed that all of the love she had lavished on Jozefat and all of the sacrifices she had made for him had been worth it. And then, the holiday came to an end.

When Jozefat and his aunt returned from their travels, nothing remained of the majestic tree except a huge jagged stump. Katarzyna stood very still, staring at the sight. When she turned to look at her nephew, her eyes told him that she understood exactly what had happened. They were full of sorrow.

"What have you done?" she cried, and with these words she collapsed to the ground and died.

Jozefat was sorry his aunt had died but he convinced himself that her death was caused by old age. And anyway, he was too overjoyed at the prospect of marrying Halina to spend much time thinking about the old woman's passing.

The young couple were wed a few weeks later. They moved into Katarzyna's home, which now belonged to Jozefat, and they were very, very happy. A year after their marriage they had a son, the next year a daughter. Everything was wonderful and they were blessed with much happiness.

But we must not forget the tree. The wood taken from the oak had been sawed into boards and the largest ones were bought by ship builders. That is how this very piece of driftwood became part of a ship. Not just any ship, mind you, but a pirate ship called *The Plunder*.

The Plunder was manned by a motley group of ruffians and scallywags—men with dark and greedy hearts. Every deed done by the crew was as dirty as they were, and you might as well know that not a man among them had any great affection for the washcloth.

The same indifference toward hygiene was true when it came to their teeth—or what remained of them, which was mostly brown and yellow stumps. These fellows weren't the least bit dashing, not like the pirates you see in movies, and girls weren't nearly as eager to kiss them.

Jozefat and Halina had been married for seven years when *The Plunder*'s captain made a fateful decision. The crew was seriously short of supplies when they happened upon another vessel that would have been an ideal target to rob, except for one thing. The ship they spotted was flying a yellow flag, known as the Yellow Jack. This was a warning for other vessels to keep their distance. It meant there was some kind of terrible sickness on board.

In spite of that, the captain gave the order for his men to attack.

"She's flying the Yellow Jack, Cap'n," shouted the lookout.

"Trickery!" roared the captain. "We'll not be taken in by it."

It was true that ships sometimes hoisted the Yellow Jack in the hope that it would keep pirates away. Sometimes it worked. Sometimes it did not. In this case, it didn't matter for there was no trickery involved. The *Yellow Jack* was waving because there was a deadly influenza on board.

It was into this pit of disease and death that the pirates went. When they realized their mistake it was already too late. Within days the sickness had spread through *The Plunder*'s crew. Everywhere you looked, men writhed in agony and those who had not fallen ill were weakened by a lack of food and fresh water.

Desperate for help, the pirate ship made its way to a small coastal town in northern Europe—the very town where Jozefat and his family lived. Before long, several of the ship's ailing crew arrived at their door brandishing swords and demanding food and care. When they took their leave several days later, Halina and the oldest boy had already taken ill. Before the month was out, mother and both children lay buried in the earth near the old oak tree's stump.

Jozefat lived out the rest of his days in loneliness and sorrow. If fate showed him any mercy, it was that he never knew the very tree he had wrongfully sold had returned and taken away everything he valued.

Theo's milky eyes stared into the distance as he finished his story, still holding the piece of wooden plank. None of us said anything for a minute. Then Theo said, "Adam, I can't keep this. It came to you for a reason."

His thin hand trembled a little as he passed it back to me.

"What's the reason?" I asked.

"That's something only *you* can find out," Theo said. "Now, would you boys care for some bread pudding?" That didn't sound like something we wanted to try, so we said thanks but we should be getting back.

I looked the piece of plank over carefully on the way to the cabins. Joey reacted to that just the way you'd expect him to. He had a few theories about why Theo had given it back to me, which were:

1. I could smack myself up the side of the head with it, in the hope that I might knock some sense into myself.
2. It was worthless, just like he'd said all along, and Theo gave it back to get out of paying the five bucks.
3. I could hold it in front of my face whenever I meet people, so my ugly puss wouldn't scare anyone.

Joey was an appreciative audience for his own jokes. But when we got to his place, he stopped making fun and said, "Want me to take that useless old thing off your hands?"

That was a surprise and I realized he wished Theo had given it to him instead of me. I told him, "Naw, I think I'll hang onto it for now."

But honestly, I would have given it to him if it would have meant he could have stayed another week or two. Plus, I told myself that having Joey there had really made up for Billy not coming. Joey was bossier and kind of mouthy sometimes, but he was fun too. It was going to be boring without him around.

Joey and his family had already left when I got up on Saturday morning. Some of the other campers were gone, too, and more headed out during the day. Keith and Monica Stillwater packed up just after lunch which is when Dad and I went over to say goodbye. Keith shook my hand and Monica hugged me and told me I was a good kid. Dad had tried to get Mom to come with us but she said there was no point.

By that afternoon there was only one other cabin besides ours that still had people in it, and there was no one to hang around with. That changed the next day, when new campers arrived. For a while, I amused myself trying to guess who'd been there before and who hadn't. Most of the folks I took as first-timers stood looking around, peering out at the bay and into the woods before they started unpacking their cars.

After a while I got bored and crossed the road to sit on a rock overlooking the water. I probably hadn't been there more than fifteen or twenty minutes when I got that neck-tickling feeling that someone was watching me. It was hard not to jerk my head around but I managed not to. If someone was there, I didn't want to act like a nervous girl in front of them. Instead, I stood up and stretched, turned around and sat down again, except this time I was facing the other way. I re-tied my shoe, which was when a flash of red moved in the trees to my left.

"You're not very good at spying," I called, just so whoever it was would know I was onto them.

For a second, nothing happened. Then a face appeared, followed by the rest of what turned out to be a girl. "I might not be good at spying," she agreed, "but I bet I can outrun you any day of the week."

"Can not," I said, even though I had no idea how fast this girl could run.

She didn't answer right away. She marched over until she was practically on top of me. Then she said, "Prove it!"

"I'd hate to make you look bad," I said. Her confidence was a bit unnerving.

"Ha!" she scoffed. "I'll race you to my cabin. It's number four." She got into a runner's stance, knees bent, face thrust forward. "One, two—"

I managed to get into position before she yelled, "THREE!" and we pushed off at the same time, sprinting across the field. I overtook her easily, and had a good lead by the time I reached the road. I paused just long enough to make sure no cars were in sight before dashing across and through the field toward the cabins.

It was the easiest race I'd ever run, so you can imagine my surprise when I rounded the corner to cabin number four and saw her sitting on the deck.

"Told you I'd beat you!" she said with a laugh.

"But you were *behind* me," I protested.

"Still beat you," she said. "Admit it."

"You beat me," I mumbled.

"So, what's your name, anyway?"

"Adam."

"Hey! Come and meet Adam," she called out.

I thought she was talking to someone in the cabin until I heard footsteps behind me. When I turned to look, I had to blink twice. Then I knew how she'd gotten there first even though I was ahead in the race. There were two of her!

"Twins!" I said.

"Right! We're the Linden twins!" said the one on the porch. "I'm Makayla and she's Mackenzie."

"How old are you? We're ten and a half and we memorize things," Mackenzie said.

"I'm *eleven*," I said. "You memorize things like what?"

"Anything that's interesting. Like, did you know that more than sixty percent of all the lakes in the world are right here in Canada?"

"Guess how many that is!" Makayla commanded.

The only lakes I knew about were the Great Lakes. I had no idea how many others there might be, but I figured it must be a lot if she wanted me to guess, so I said, "A thousand?"

"A *thousand*," Mackenzie scoffed. "Wrong!"

"Two or three *million*!" said Makayla. "No one knows the exact number."

"We know a lot of stuff like that," Mackenzie bragged.

"I know things, too," I said.

The twins gave each other a look that said they doubted it, but before they could challenge me, their cabin door opened and a man stepped out. He had on a chef-style apron and was carrying a metal tray with piles of wieners and buns on it.

"Almost time for the big barbeque!" he said. That's when he noticed me. "Hello, there. Would you like to help out?"

"Sure he would, Dad," one of the twins said. They were now standing together and I didn't have a clue which one was Makayla and which one was Mackenzie. "He's Adam and his family is staying in cabin number ten."

"Excellent!" their father said. I didn't know if he meant because I was a camper, or because I'd just been volunteered to help out doing who knows what.

"Come on, Adam," said a twin. "We have to invite all the people in all the cabins to come for a hotdog."

"It's our family tradition!" said the other twin.

"We started it the first year we came to Schooner Point," said their dad. "It's a great way to get to know your neighbours."

"Let's go to your place first, Adam."

I didn't have much enthusiasm for that suggestion. It was hard to say what kind of mood my mom would be in. If she was having a good painting day, it would be fine. That always cheered her up, but it hadn't been happening much since we'd started our holiday.

Unfortunately, there was no time to think of an excuse. The girls were already down the steps and heading toward my place. I took a breath and started to follow, but Mr. Linden's hand on my shoulder stopped me.

"Makayla has a little scar above her left eyebrow," he whispered. "I know it's hard to tell the girls apart."

I thought it was cool of him to tell me that, which made me hope my folks would agree to come and eat one of his hotdogs. I hurried to catch up with the girls and then told them to wait outside the cabin, in case Mom was busy.

"Why would your mom be busy on vacation?" asked Mackenzie.

"She's an artist," I explained. "And actually, my dad is working on his laptop a lot of the time, too." I hurried inside before they asked anything else. Mom was seated in front of the easel, staring glumly at the same painting she'd been working on for over a week.

"I might as well face it," she said, "There's no life in my work anymore."

Dad glanced over from the table, where he was reading. "Maybe it's time you took a break—did something other than paint," he said. "They say a change is as good as a rest."

Mom scowled.

"Guess what!" I said, "Makayla and Mackenzie's father is making hotdogs and everybody's invited!"

"Who are you talking about?" Mom asked.

"They're twins. Their family is here for a couple of weeks."

Dad put his book down and stood up. "Sounds like a great idea to me. What do you say, June?"

Mom glanced at her painting. "All right," she said, though she didn't exactly sound keen about it.

"It's at cabin four," said a voice in the doorway. "Come on, Adam, we have to invite *everyone*!"

"These girls sure are bossy," I muttered. But I went.

I trailed along behind Makayla and Mackenzie as they went from cabin to cabin inviting people to the barbeque. Almost everyone agreed to come. I was pretty much useless but they kept dragging me along and there was no reason not to go. Actually, I thought it was a good chance to find out if there were any other kids there that week who were around my age. By which I mean boys.

It didn't look good. Most of the other kids were too young. And then, at cabin one, there was a guy who was about sixteen. Mackenzie was in the middle of telling him about the hotdogs when he stepped back and shut the door right in her face. And I can tell you, that girl never missed a beat. She turned to Makayla with a strange kind of smile and said, "Well, I guess he's going to have to pay for *that*."

It was the coolest thing I'd ever heard a girl say.

Before we could walk away, the door opened again and a woman stuck her head out. "Don't mind Nevin," she said. "Tell your father we'll be along. Some of us, anyway."

There was already a crowd around the Linden's cabin when we got back. I was looking forward to having a hotdog—maybe a couple if there were extras—but the menu had gotten a lot bigger. In fact, the place looked like there'd been an explosion of things to eat. Everybody had brought something with them, and extra picnic tables had been carried over while Mr. Linden poked away at the barbeque. People passed around paper plates and napkins and spread out the food they'd brought. Besides the hotdogs, there were salads and pickles, doughnuts and cookies, and fruit. Pop and juice and milk were gathered in a corner beside paper cups. It was like a party.

Nevin's mom and dad came along and, after a while, he wandered over like he wanted to ask them something. Only, he forgot to wander back to his own cabin afterward. He sat in the grass off to one side working his way through a plate that was heaped with about as much food as it could possibly hold.

Makayla's eyes narrowed when she saw him. "Look at that," she grumbled.

"I see it," muttered Mackenzie. "Who does he think he is—Joey Chestnut?"

"*Who*?" I said.

The girls gave each other a look like they felt sorry for me for knowing so little about the world.

"A hotdog eating champion," Mackenzie explained. "He's won a bunch of times."

"How many hotdogs can he eat?" I asked.

"More than sixty," said Makayla. "In ten minutes."

I couldn't tell if she was joking or not but it sounded impossible—and painful. I once gobbled three hamburgers plus cake and ice cream at a community picnic and my stomach hurt for hours.

There was no point in asking them if it was true. I could see that they weren't interested in talking about this hotdog guy anymore. Instead, I moved a bit closer because they had their heads together and they were whispering and giggling. It made me nervous even though I was almost positive they were talking about Nevin.

Makayla noticed. "Are you trying to spy on our conversation?" she demanded.

"Kind of," I admitted. It seemed pointless to deny it. They made me feel as if they could see right into my head.

Mackenzie laughed. "At least you're honest," she said. She nodded for me to join them.

"He can be the photographer," she said to Makayla, who seemed to like the idea. "Here's my camera. Be ready to get some pictures of Nevin."

"Doing what?" I asked.

"Just find a good place and be ready," Makayla told me. "You'll know when."

I made my way to a spot on the deck where I had a decent view of Nevin. I sat down with my legs hanging over the side and tried not to make it obvious that I was watching him. He was piling stuff into himself pretty fast. He'd gorged his way through half of the mountain of food on his plate in the time it took me to eat a single hotdog. By then, I was wondering if the girls had given up whatever they'd been planning.

They hadn't.

It was Mackenzie who climbed up on one of the picnic table seats and got everyone's attention. "We're having a contest!" she hollered. "The first person who licks their own elbow will win an amazing prize! You'll have thirty seconds, and it's not easy, so start NOW!"

I was awfully tempted to try it myself but I knew whatever they were planning must have something to do with this elbow-licking business, so I kept my eye on Nevin. Sure enough, he took the bait—put his plate down and went for it. I got a few pictures of him with his arm bent and his tongue stuck out, straining to reach it. And he wasn't the only one who tried. It was pretty funny to watch.

"Time's up!" Mackenzie shouted. "Sorry, everybody but there are no prize winners today. Better luck next time."

Nevin hardly missed a beat. He shrugged, grabbed his plate, and went right back to eating. At the same time, Makayla appeared behind me and whispered, "Okay, get ready," which was my first clue that something else was going to happen.

It took about three seconds and then I saw Nevin pause and look closer at his plate. His free hand reached down and grasped something. He lifted it up and I zoomed in for some close-ups as his face went from shock to horror.

"*Akkk!*" he yelled, jumping to his feet and gagging.

"What's wrong?" Mackenzie asked, rushing to his side. That didn't take long since she'd positioned herself behind him, just a few feet away.

He looked at her wildly. "I ate half a worm!" he said. He held up his hand and I could see what appeared to be the other half of the worm dangling from his fingers.

"Let me see," she said, snatching it from him. She looked it over. "I guess you did," she agreed. "But don't worry. You *probably* won't die."

Nevin seemed to lose his appetite after that. A few minutes later he headed back to his own cabin, holding his stomach and looking a little green.

While the girls inspected the pictures I'd taken, I had a question for them.

"What was the prize, if somebody had licked their elbow in time?"

"It's impossible. No one can do it," Mackenzie said. "That was just a distraction so I could toss this onto his plate." She reached into her pocket and pulled out the half worm.

"It's not even real," Makayla told me. "That's why we had to get it from him quick, before he realized it was rubber."

I was starting to realize that these girls were geniuses. And I couldn't help thinking that it was lucky I'd been a good sport about the trick they played on me when we first met.

Thinking he'd eaten a hunk of worm didn't do anything to improve Nevin's disposition. Every time we saw him over the next few days, he went out of his way to glare at us and, if we were within hearing distance, he'd mutter something uncomplimentary about kids. Like he was so old compared to us.

The girls found it entertaining, and went out of *their* way to cross paths with him as much as possible. I didn't find it quite so funny. It looked to me like Nevin had a mean streak, and that made me a little nervous.

I was worried that he'd figured out we were behind the whole worm incident. The one he thought was real and believed he'd spent his first day at the cabin digesting. If he was onto us, it seemed likely he was plotting some sort of revenge. I mentioned this to the twins.

"He probably is," said Makayla. She smiled.

Mackenzie grinned at her sister and said, "Lotsa luck to him, then." And would you believe they actually laughed, like it was a huge joke this nasty hulk of a teenager might be after us?

These girls had nerves of steel. I hate to say it, but I felt braver when I was around them. Nothing seemed to bother that pair. And for girls, they were okay to hang out with. You know, since there were no boys and I didn't have a choice. Their habit of showing off all the stuff they knew could get annoying, but then some of it was pretty interesting.

One afternoon we were throwing a Frisbee in the field across the road when a huge Monarch butterfly came flitting through the air. Mackenzie made us stop what we were doing, so it wouldn't get dinged by accident.

"Don't you think it's beautiful, Adam?" she said, gazing at it all girl-faced.

"It's okay," I answered. I mean, it was just a butterfly.

"I bet you don't know what the original name was for a butterfly," she said.

Of course, I didn't. Anyway, it seemed that she'd turned a little grumpy, probably because I hadn't swooned over the silly thing. I shrugged, so she'd see I wasn't exactly excited about whatever the answer was.

"Flutterby!" Makayla blurted.

"Huh?"

"That's the butterfly's original name. Flutterby."

"Really?" I have to admit, I found that a *little* bit interesting. And it was the kind of thing that was easy to remember. The girls were always reciting numbers and figures that I'd never have been able to keep track of, but this was a cinch.

"Hey, you know what's got a really fun *scientific* name?" Mackenzie asked. She seemed to be restored to good humour. "A gorilla!"

"Oh, yeah? What is it?"

"I'll give you *three* guesses!" she said. Then she and Makayla looked at each other and giggled.

I'm not great at guessing games. It was obvious that there was a clue in the way she'd emphasized *three* but it didn't exactly help me figure out the answer. Besides, I knew that anything I said would come out sounding lame. So I refused to guess and just said I had no idea.

"Gorilla Gorilla Gorilla," Mackenzie squealed.

It took me a couple of seconds to understand that "Gorilla Gorilla Gorilla" was the scientific name. It was a kind of cool thing to know and I was hoping they might have some more— especially if they were that easy to remember. But Makayla had something else in mind.

"Let's go see your mom," she said.

"*My* mom?" I asked. Which was kind of dumb, since I was the only one there whose mother wasn't also her mother.

"Sure. I want to see what she's painting," Makayla said.

By now you know that this was a pretty touchy subject with my mother. I tried to tell them that I didn't think dropping in on her for some art chat was such a great idea but it was hopeless. You could stand on your head and shoot flames out your toes easier than you could stop the twins once they decided they were going to do something.

I followed along behind them hoping my mom wouldn't say anything too rude. I didn't think they'd sneak a rubber worm into her food or anything if she did, I just didn't want them to know how Mom gets when her art is giving her trouble. Or, as my dad says (though, not in front of her) when she's in one of her creative dithers. That makes Mom seem kind of mean, which isn't what she's really like, and I didn't want the twins getting the wrong idea.

When they got to my cabin they stopped and waited for me to lead them inside. I was still trying to think of a way to stop the visit as I stuck my head in and said, "Are you busy, Mom?"

My best hope was that Mom would say she was and that would be the end of it, but she didn't.

"I'm about as busy as any other day," she said, looking over from her usual spot in front of her easel.

I was trying to think of what to do next when, from behind me, Makayla hissed, "Ask if we can come in!"

"Can the twins come in?" I asked obediently.

Mom gave a little wave with her hand so I stepped inside and the girls burst in after me. They went straight over to the easel and stood looking at the painting-in-progress. Although, there hadn't been much actual progress for the last week or so, as far as I could tell.

"That's the world's longest covered bridge," I explained. "It's in Hartland, where we live."

"That's awesome!" said Mackenzie. "How come you never mentioned it before?"

I didn't want to admit that I thought they'd find it lame in comparison to all the facts and world records and curiosities they knew about. Luckily, they hardly ever wait for an answer when they ask a question and this was no exception.

"This is amazing," Makayla said, leaning closer to the painting. "Don't you think it's amazing, Mackenzie?"

"Totally," Mackenzie agreed, sounding awestruck. "It must be awesome to be able to paint like that."

"I know we probably can't afford it, but how much would this cost, when it's finished?" Makayla asked.

When I looked over, I was alarmed to see that Mom's eyes were filling with tears. But they weren't upset tears, like I thought at first. She reached out and tugged the twins over to her and put an arm around each of them. Then she started laughing and she kissed each of them on the forehead. Of course, being girls, they didn't seem to mind.

Once Mom got herself under control, she told them that when the painting was finished, she was going to give it to them as a gift. Then there was a bunch of squealing, followed by more hugging and sniffling. Joey was lucky he got out of here before he had to see that kind of performance, that's for sure.

I was happy because the twins had cheered Mom up. But there was more. Mackenzie, who'd plastered herself to Mom's side, lifted her eyes from the painting to look up in Mom's face.

"How can you paint this when the bridge isn't here for you to see?" she asked.

"Memory," Mom told her. "I've painted it so many times that I can see it with my mind's eye."

"Is the bridge the only thing you paint?" Mackenzie said.

"It's what the tourists want," Mom said.

"If I could do something this fantastic," Mackenzie said, "I'd paint *everything*. I'd paint the trees and the river. I'd paint that chair and this cabin and a bird soaring through the sky, and—"

Her voice broke off and she stood, staring past all of us, into some place only she could see. She stayed like that, frozen in place, until Mom burst out laughing. That got everyone's attention. It didn't sound quite right, not like her normal laugh when something strikes her as funny. There was a bit of a crazy sound to it, enough that my dad came hurrying in from wherever he'd been.

"Are you all right, June?" he asked.

"I'm better than all right!" Mom said. "Do you see this?" she asked, pointing at the easel. "This is the last bridge I'm going to paint for a long, long time. I may *never* paint another bridge. I've been working in chains, but no more! This child has opened my eyes."

Then she crossed the room, threw her arms around him and gave him a big old kiss. The girls looked at me and giggled and raised their eyebrows up and down a couple of times, which made me about as nervous as I've ever been.

12

The painting of the bridge was finished when I got up the next morning and Mom was humming while she made scrambled eggs and toast. She threw me a smile and poured me a glass of orange juice. She looked happier than I'd seen her in a long time.

I knew it was the twins—how they'd reacted to the painting and what they'd said. I was glad but it puzzled me a little too. I seemed to remember my dad saying practically the same things, with no result at all. Maybe what got through to Mom was the look on Mackenzie's face when she was talking about all the things she'd paint, if she could.

After we'd eaten, Mom asked Dad if he wanted to go for a walk, which was another new thing. Since we'd gotten to Schooner Point, she'd mostly spent her days inside, in front of the easel. It seemed that was going to change, too, because she asked Dad to set it up for her in the field looking out over the water.

"I don't know when I stopped looking at the world," she said. "I feel as though I've had blinders on for the longest time."

Dad hugged her then and I high-tailed it on out of there before they started up with a repeat of yesterday's mush. There should be rules about kissing in front of your kids.

The twins were already outside, and I almost blurted out that their painting was ready. I'd already said, "Guess what?" when I realized I should leave it to Mom to do in her own time and way. Of course, by then, the girls were looking at me inquisitively.

"What?" they asked together. I had to think fast.

"There's an old guy up the beach who's blind and he pays five bucks for driftwood, if he can use it," I said. "He makes stuff out of it. And he tells cool stories about where it came from."

They had a few questions but as soon as they could tell I wasn't making it up, they were eager to go exploring.

"Which way have you looked lately?" Makayla asked when we got to the shore.

"That way—Theo's house is in that direction, too," I said.

The girls pointed out that it made sense to explore in the other direction in that case, and we turned left and headed along. It was slow going with those two. They had to stop and examine every shell and shiny stone they saw.

"We should have brought a bag to collect things," Mackenzie said after a while. "Adam could have carried it and we could have filled it with treasures."

"We'll remember the next time," Makayla said. They both seemed to think that was a great idea. Nobody asked what *I* thought of it.

We walked what seemed to be a long way without any luck. It was thirst that made us decide to give up and turn back, since none of us had brought anything to drink. That gave the girls more brilliant ideas about things I could carry the next time. By the sounds of it, they were planning to turn me into some kind of human pack mule to lug around their water and snacks and whatever they scavenged along the way. I figured it was lucky I was there to hear all of this, so I could think of an excuse not to go with them again.

We were in sight of the shore area that's across from the cabins when we saw someone heading our way. I realized, with a sinking feeling, that it was Nevin. His movements struck me as menacing, and as he got closer I could see a look of pure gloating on his face.

I turned to see if there was anyone behind us, but there was no one else on the shore. The girls were looking straight at Nevin, but they obviously hadn't clued in to the fact that this encounter meant trouble. I was about to whisper a warning to them, but he spoke up before I had a chance.

"Didn't expect to see *me*, did you?"

"We didn't expect to *not* see you either," said Makayla.

"To be honest, we weren't out here giving you a whole lot of thought," added Mackenzie.

It was like they were *trying* to make things worse.

"I'm not dumb, you know," Nevin said, his voice getting louder. "I know you guys put that worm in my food."

"True," Makayla agreed.

"So you admit it!" Nevin said, glowering.

"Yes—that's what 'true' means," Mackenzie pointed out.

"I hope you don't think you're going to get away with it," Nevin thundered. "Because you're not!"

"What did you have in mind?" Mackenzie asked. She sounded curious but not one bit afraid. I was wondering why neither of them was telling him the worm hadn't been real and that he hadn't actually eaten any. It was all I could do not to blurt it out myself, but I knew the girls would think I was a coward if I did.

"How would you all like to eat a little sand?" Nevin asked.

"None for me, thanks," said Makayla.

"Oh, there will be some for you all right," Nevin

said. "There'll be some for all of you! And that's just the beginning."

"You're going to make us eat sand?" Mackenzie asked, like she just wanted to be sure.

"That's right," Nevin said. I could see he was puzzled why the twins seemed so calm. To tell the truth, so was I.

"That doesn't sound like a very smart idea to me," Mackenzie told him. "I know one thing. I wouldn't go around feeding sand to a cop's daughters, that's for sure."

All of the triumph drained right out of Nevin's face. He flapped his mouth and sputtered a few times before his voice cooperated enough for him to speak.

"I didn't mean I was going to do it—right now. I was just giving you a warning. But you'd better not mess with me again."

The girls smiled at him so innocently you'd have sworn they were a couple of angels out for a stroll by the water. Nevin scowled but he didn't say another word. He turned around and hurried back the way he'd come. It only took a couple of minutes before he reached the path up to the cabins and disappeared from sight.

"I didn't know your dad was a cop," I said.

"He's not," said Makayla.

"He's a podiatrist," Mackenzie added.

"But you said—"

"I didn't say *my* father was a cop. All I said was

that I wouldn't feed sand to a cop's daughters—which I *wouldn't*," Mackenzie said. "Anyway, I'm thirsty! Let's go get a drink!"

———

A few days went by before we decided to go exploring again, and this time we found a pretty decent-sized branch along the shore that stretched toward Theo's place. It must have come in with a recent tide because it was sitting out in the open with seaweed still clinging to it.

We picked the limp, wet strands from it and brushed off the sand. That reminded me of something my dad had told me.

"Did you know that they use sand to make glass?" I asked.

"Sure," Makayla said, crushing my hope that this might be something new—and interesting—to them. She scooped up a handful and let it run through her fingers.

"I wonder how many grains of sand it takes to make a water glass," Mackenzie said.

"Maybe a million," I said, "or a billion."

"There's a big difference between a million and a billon," Makayla said. For some reason, she looked kind of cross about it.

"I know that," I said.

"In that case, how long do you think it takes for a million seconds to go by?" she asked.

"A year?" It was a wild guess but I was hoping I might get lucky.

"Nope. About eleven and a half days," Mackenzie said.

"And how long do you think it takes for a *billion* seconds to go by?" Makayla asked.

"Probably about three or four months," I guessed, hoping I was closer this time.

"Almost thirty-two *years*!" the girls shouted together.

I have to admit I was pretty surprised. And I was hoping I could remember it to impress my friends when I got back home. (I knew Billy would have found it cool, so it was too bad for him we weren't friends anymore.) I repeated it in my head the rest of the way to Theo's place.

When we got there, I introduced the twins. Theo's face lit up with a great big smile as they started their usual jabbering.

"We were just teaching Adam the difference between a million and a billion," Mackenzie told him.

"Is that so, now?" Theo said.

"It sure is. We try to teach Adam a few things every day. He doesn't know *nearly* as much as we do."

"That's because we collect interesting infor-mation," Mackenzie added. "Hardly *anyone* our age knows all the things we do."

"My, my," said Theo.

"But, I hope you don't think we're bragging," Makayla said.

"We wouldn't do that," Mackenzie claimed. "We're just stating the facts."

Theo chuckled.

"Oh! And guess what!" Makayla said then. "We found a piece of driftwood."

"And we brought it here for you," Mackenzie said. She nodded at me, like that was my cue to pass it over, since, naturally, it had been my job to carry it.

"I told them about how you collect it," I added, as Theo reached out to take hold of the piece of wood.

I could tell that the twins were excited as they waited to see if Theo would have a story about the driftwood, like I'd said he would.

He didn't let me down. Within a few minutes, Theo's voice was taking us to another time and place.

13

THE MOUNTAIN MAHOGANY

This fine branch comes from a tree called the Mountain Mahogany. The tree it was part of grew before the white man came to North America, back when the native peoples lived by the laws of their ancestors. There were many tribes and one of those was called the Southern Paiute. They were a peaceful people who lived off what the land provided.

One of the Paiute tribes lived near the Great Basin in what is now known as Utah, in the United States of America.

In this tribe there was a young brave who was known as Little Spear. Little Spear wanted to go along with the men when they hunted for food but he was too young. When they were preparing to leave, he would beg and make a pleading face. The answer was, "No." Then he would make a sad face, and later on, an angry face. None of those faces helped. The answer was still, "No," and he was left behind.

Little Spear's mother watched her son stomp about and grumble that he was almost a man. He was as straight as an arrow and growing tall but his body was still young and slender. It was not yet the body of a hunter. Even so, his mother's heart was stirred by his longing and his misery.

"Little Spear grows restless," she told his father as the sun fell from the sky one evening. "I fear that his impatience may make him bitter."

Little Spear's father said nothing but he pondered her words. The next time that the men gathered to hunt, he called his son to him.

"It is time for you to begin your journey," he said. "If you will be a hunter someday, you must learn to be still and watch. Are you ready for this step?"

Little Spear nodded. He listened carefully as his father gave him his instructions. At daylight of the first morning after the men had been gone for three sunsets, he must go and climb into the branches of a grey tree at the top of the nearest hill. From there, he was to watch for the hunters returning. As soon as he spotted them, he must run back to tell the others. In this way, by the time the men reached their home, preparations for cooking the meal would be completed.

"It is an important job," his father told him. "I know you will do it well."

Little Spear was proud to have a new responsibility. On the third morning after the hunters left he set out for the hill and climbed into the tree, just as his father had instructed him. Before long, a coyote came along. Little Spear was not afraid even though the coyote was known as a trickster and a troublemaker among the Paiute people. He knew the coyote could not reach him in the tree.

The coyote sat down very close to the tree. He did not seem to notice that Little Spear was there. Hours passed and the task of watching the horizon for signs of the men made the young brave's eyes tired and sleepy. He wished he could climb down to the ground to limber up and chase away the drowsiness.

"Coyote!" he said. "Why don't you move along somewhere else?"

The coyote looked at him with sad eyes. "I will go if you do not want me here," it said.

Little Spear thought it must be a trick, but the coyote made its way along a path toward the river. When it was out of sight, Little Spear climbed down and stretched his arms and legs. It felt good, but he was haunted by the coyote's sadness.

The next day, Little Spear again took his place in the tree. The excitement he'd felt over his new job was fading like the mist on a summer morning. It was difficult not to think of how pleasant his days had been before he had been given this new responsibility. It wasn't only the discomfort of sitting in the tree for long hours that he minded—it was the boredom. The worst thing was, he knew that if the hunt did not go well it could be many more sunrises before the men returned.

On this day, Little Spear had not been in the tree very long when the coyote made its appearance.

"Hello, friend," it said as it settled down near the tree.

"You are not my friend," Little Spear said.

"Who told you that I am not?" asked the coyote.

"Your teeth are sharp and quick to destroy," Little Spear answered. "This truth is well known among my people."

"That is most peculiar," said the coyote. "For I have been taught to fear your kind."

Little Spear was still thinking about this when the coyote spoke again.

"What are you doing in the tree?" it asked.

"I am watching for the hunters to return," Little Spear answered. "Perhaps the next time I will go with them."

"Why watch from the tree?" asked the coyote. "You would be much more comfortable here. And you can see almost as far."

"My father told me to watch from the tree," Little Spear said firmly. The coyote gave him a sympathetic look and said nothing more. Later, when Little Spear suggested it might be time for the coyote to leave, it trotted off with a friendly wave of its tail.

The next day, the coyote was back again. It said, "Good day, friend," before stretching out flat on the ground. Little Spear could not help but notice how relaxed and comfortable the coyote looked, especially when it rolled onto its back and writhed a little in the warm sand.

"Are you sure your father wanted you to sit up there the entire time?" the coyote asked.

Little Spear tried to remember his father's words. He wondered if he'd made a mistake. Perhaps he only needed to go up now and then. After all, as the coyote had pointed out already, he could see almost as far from the hilltop itself.

For the next three days the coyote continued to visit. He told Little Spear stories about his family, and about what his childhood had been like. He shared coyote legends of great feats of strength and courage. They were not so very different from some of the stories Little Spear had heard about his own ancestors.

The best story the coyote told was of the time long ago when their ancestors had all been friends. They lived and hunted together, and when there was trouble for one, the other rose up to help. "That time is no more," the coyote said sadly.

"Perhaps it will come again someday," Little

Spear suggested, but his visitor only shook his head, got to his feet, and ambled away.

The next day, the coyote did not come. Little Spear watched and waited in vain, and the day dragged by more slowly than any other. On the day after that, when he saw the coyote heading slowly toward him, his spirits lifted.

"Hello!" he called.

"I have come to say goodbye," said the coyote when he reached the hilltop.

"Why?" asked the boy.

"Because you will always see me as your enemy." The coyote's head dropped low.

Little Spear's heart began to hurt at those words. He spoke quickly. "That was before," he told the coyote. "Now that I know you, I see that you are a friend."

The coyote looked at him warily. "How do I know you are telling me the truth?" he asked.

Little Spear knew what he must do. He climbed down from the tree and crossed the few steps to where the coyote sat. He smiled and kneeled beside his new friend. He put his arms around the coyote's neck and laid his face against the coarse fur.

Suddenly, a low growl came from deep in the coyote's throat. His head turned toward the boy and Little Spear looked into the creature's eyes for the first time. In those yellow pools, Little Spear saw cunning and triumph, and he knew he had been deceived.

What came next happened so fast that the young brave barely had time to react. The coyote spun, its sharp, white teeth flashing as its jaws opened and snapped on Little Spear's arm.

The boy struggled to his feet, striking back with his free hand. He slammed it hard on the coyote's nose. That made the coyote yelp and Little Spear pulled his injured arm free and leapt toward the safety of the tree. He scrambled up as the coyote reached the trunk and lunged toward him.

This was the day that Little Spear discovered a great truth. The most dangerous enemy of all is the one who comes disguised as a friend.

I knew the twins weren't shy about speaking their mind so I was a bit nervous about what they might say when Theo's tale was finished. One look at their faces told me I had nothing to worry about. Their eyes were shining and it was clear they were spellbound by the story.

"That was fantastic!" Makayla said. "It must be incredible to be able to touch something and know all about it that way."

Theo smiled and his head turned toward her, even though he couldn't see her face. "I consider it a rare and wonderful gift. Never had it as a young fellow. It's only in the last few years that I've been able to feel the story from a piece of driftwood in my hands."

"Well, it's amazing!" Mackenzie said.

It struck me that the twins' voices sounded a

lot like they had the day they talked to my mom about her paintings. They were breathless and excited, as if they'd made the greatest discovery of their lives. And even though it seemed like a girl thing, I couldn't help thinking it must be fun to go around being that enthusiastic about stuff. No wonder they remember so many things—it all *matters* to them.

"Little Spear should have known he could never trust a coyote," Makayla said suddenly. She sounded cross about it, which almost made me laugh.

"The coyote was pretending to be his friend," I reminded her. "Little Spear got tricked into believing it."

"Are there any coyotes around here?" Mackenzie asked Theo.

"That kind of coyote is everywhere," Theo told her. "But they don't always look like coyotes. Sometimes they're in disguise."

"As what?" I said.

"Wolves in sheep's clothing," Theo said.

"You're talking about *people*, aren't you?" Makayla asked. Theo nodded.

"I know someone like that," I said. The image of Billy's traitorous face rose in my mind. "My friend was supposed to come here with me, but he backed out at the last minute."

"He turned on you, just like the coyote did to Little Spear!" Makayla said.

"Yeah, but he won't fool me again," I told them.

"Because we're not friends anymore."

"He showed his true colours," Mackenzie declared. "Right, Theo?"

"A false friend always reveals himself in the end," Theo said. At the same time, he pulled his wallet from his pocket. Opening it, he drew out a five dollar bill and held it toward us.

"Goodness, no!" Mackenzie said.

"Isn't this a five?" Theo asked.

"No. I mean, yes, it *is* a five. But we don't want it," Makayla said.

"The story was *so good*!" Mackenzie said. "We don't want money, too. Right, Adam?"

"Right," I agreed. I suddenly felt foolish for ever taking money from him.

"Well, if you aren't the best kids I ever heard tell of!" Theo said. He smiled and tucked the money back into his wallet. Then he asked, "Would any of you care for a snack? I have some frogs here."

"Yes, please!" the twins said.

I said I'd have one but it worried me, not knowing if the frog Theo was going to serve us was a chocolate and coconut cookie like my mom makes, or if it might be something that involved an actual frog, since Theo's snacks aren't always what you're expecting. It was a relief to see him return with a plate of the kind I was used to.

"These are great; did you make them?" Makayla asked after she'd swallowed a bite and was about to take a second.

"Oh, no. My daughter comes over a couple times a week," he said. "She bakes and cooks and cleans. Does more than she should, but that will end soon."

"Why? Is she moving away?" Mackenzie asked.

"Nope, but I won't need her as much once I can see again," he told her.

"You're going to be able to *see* again?" I said. Really, I nearly hollered it. I had no idea how Theo could sit there as calm as could be with news that exciting.

"That's right," Theo said, looking oddly gloomy. "The doctor is going to operate and remove the cataracts."

"When?" I asked.

"Early in August," Theo said. He didn't look pleased, the way you'd expect from someone who was going to get his sight back.

"Are you nervous?" Makayla asked.

"Well, now, I feel foolish to admit it but the truth is, I'm scared silly. I have what they call a phobia about hospitals and operations and such. That's one of the reasons I've held off so long."

Mackenzie moved closer and took hold of Theo's bony old hand with both of hers. She looked up into his face.

"Here," she said, "I'm really brave, so I'm giving you some of my courage." Theo's lip trembled and for the first time since he'd started talking about it, he managed a smile.

A bit later, on our way back to the cabins, Makayla suddenly stopped walking and turned to us. "Did you ever think about what it would be like to be blind?" she asked.

Before Mackenzie or I could answer, she clapped her hands over her eyes. "Cover your eyes!" she commanded.

"Can't we just close them?" I asked. That made her take her hands away from hers and look at me like she couldn't quite believe my nerve.

"You might open them by mistake," she said. "Blinking is automatic you know—like breathing."

"That's true," Mackenzie said. "Did you know that you blink your eyes about eleven thousand times a day?"

Of course I didn't know that. I never knew any of the things the twins knew. They went around blasting out bits of trivia like miniature game-show hosts.

"Never mind that," Makayla said impatiently. "Just do what I said."

I shut my eyes and obediently put my hands over them. We all stood very still for a few minutes, then Makayla spoke again.

"It's so dark," she said.

"Do you think that's what it's like for Theo?" Mackenzie asked. Her voice was barely more than a whisper.

"No, it isn't," I said. I sensed movement from

the girls so I peeked out through a couple of fingers. They'd both dropped their hands and opened their eyes, so I did the same. They were staring at me, waiting for me to explain.

"It's like the world is blurry and fuzzy. He sort of sees shapes but he can't tell what anything is."

"How do you know?"

"He told me," I said, enjoying the moment. It felt good to be the one who knew something they didn't know. For a change. "He said he already had poor vision before, and when he got cataracts they made it worse and worse."

"I'm glad," Mackenzie said. "I mean, I'm glad it's not all dark for him all the time. Of course I'm not glad that he has cataracts."

I noticed there was a little dark smudge on her nose. Probably chocolate from the frog she ate at Theo's place. I'm not sure why, but there was something really cute about it. Then she noticed me looking.

"What are you staring at?"

"Nothing." I felt my neck and cheeks get hot, which somehow made me blurt, "Your face is dirty."

"Who cares, weirdo?" she said. "Let's go."

When we got back to the field across from our cabins, my mother was there, standing motionless behind her easel. Even her hand, holding a paintbrush, was paused in the air. It looked like she'd been frozen in place—like her battery had run out.

The twins hurried over to her, which seemed to break the spell. Mom's hand dropped to her side and she burst into a huge smile.

"Hello, girls!" she said.

"I'm here too, Mom," I grumbled.

"I know you are, sweetie," she said.

"Come see this, *sweetie*," Makayla said. She and Mackenzie giggled like that was hilarious.

I tried not to react because I knew that would only encourage them. That was easy to do because when I reached the painting, I found myself gaping at the canvas in front of me.

Mom had been painting the bay that stretched out from where we were standing, and it was like nothing she'd ever done before. I could feel the warmth of the sun glinting on the water's surface, the cold of its depths below. It almost seemed as if it was *breathing*—swollen with a life pulse I'd never seen in her paintings of our famous bridge over the Saint John River.

When I glanced at the girls, I could see that they were as mesmerized as I was. That didn't stop Makayla from turning to me with a big grin and saying, "Pretty amazing isn't it, *sweetie*?"

"It's awesome, Mom," I said, ignoring Makayla. "Can we keep it?"

I'd never have opened my mouth if I'd known saying that was going to make Mom burst into tears and start mauling me right out in an open field, that's for sure. She hugged me and cried and kept saying I'd never asked anything like that before and I had no idea what it meant to her. Even the girls, who think Mom is great, looked a bit embarrassed at how she was going on.

Once she got herself under control, Mom said she thought she'd wrap it up for the day. She said other things too, about the world being fresh and new and her heart singing and stuff like that. I pretty much tuned it out.

"We can help you take your stuff back," Mackenzie said when Mom had finally finished her speech.

"Maybe the easel," Mom said. "I'll carry the painting, and that nice young man is coming to help me with the supply box. He carried it here for me earlier."

"What nice young man?" I asked.

"That one," Mom said, nodding toward a figure heading our way from the campground.

I blinked and stared but I still didn't quite believe what I was seeing.

It was Nevin.

The twins seemed just as surprised as I was when Nevin showed up to carry Mom's supply box back to our cabin. Even stranger was the way he stood there and studied the painting we'd all been admiring. I watched his eyes move over it, taking in every detail.

He didn't say anything when he was finished, he just looked at Mom and nodded. She smiled and said, "I have some canvases with me that I won't be needing. If you're interested, you can come along tomorrow and use one."

"Maybe," he said. He didn't sound too interested.

It wasn't until I was eating supper later that I thought about Theo again.

"Hey," I said, "Guess what I found out from Theo today! He's having an operation to fix his eyes in a few weeks. He'll be able to see again."

"Boy, oh boy, that's just *wonderful*!" Dad said.

Mom got wet-eyed and clasped her hands in front of her. "It's the summer for miracles," she said.

———

There were no miracles the next day, that's for sure. I woke up feeling sick to my stomach and hardly made it to the bathroom in time. Any hope that it was a one-time thing disappeared with a repeat performance about fifteen minutes later, which was when Mom sent me back to bed.

"It's a bug—probably one of those twenty-four hour viruses," she said. "Best thing to do is rest and wait it out."

Mom is pretty practical when any of us are sick. She doesn't believe in fussing over a person just because their nose is running or they're barfing or whatever. I didn't even know that some mothers did things differently until one time when Billy stayed at our place for a weekend. His folks were away, so he had no choice but to stay put when he came down with some sort of flu. First thing he did was start complaining.

"Your mom is mean," he moaned.

I didn't like him saying that—she is my mom after all—but I'd heard her tell my father he had an airborne virus and I didn't want to get too close to his air to defend her. "What do you mean by that?" I asked from across the room.

"Here I am, sick as a dog, and what's your mom doing? Nothing!" The outrage of it made tears start up in his eyes as his head sank back onto the pillow. His mutt, Bailey, lay beside him, face flat on the floor, looking mournfully at the ceiling and thumping his tail in a slow rhythm against the side of the bed. It was hard to say which one of them looked sadder.

"What's my mom *supposed* to do?" I asked.

"Sit by me and wipe my face with a cool facecloth, for starters," he said. "I could have a fever for all she knows. She never even checked my temperature or nothing."

"She put her hand on your forehead," I reminded him. "That's how my mom checks for a fever."

"That's not very scientific," Billy said. "My mom uses a thermometer. And she brings me ice chips and soup and ginger ale with the fizz stirred out of it."

"My mom will get you an extra blanket if you need it," I said.

"Does she warm it up in the dryer first?" he asked.

"I don't think so."

"Well, does she know how to fluff a pillow?"

"I'm not real sure," I said.

Billy moaned again. "This is awful," he said. "Here I am, sicker than two dogs, and I have to make do with someone else's mother who doesn't even know how to fluff a pillow."

By the end of that weekend, the list of things

Billy said his mom did for him when he was sick was so long it would have taken a team of moms working around the clock to keep up with it all.

Like I already said, my mom isn't like that, so I was pretty much left on my own that day. Not that she ignored me completely. She popped her head into my room a few times while I lay there feeling wretched.

"How you doing, sport?" she asked. "You'll be right as rain in no time." After lunch she told me she'd be in the field, painting.

"Your dad is here if you need anything."

It's true that Dad was around most of the day but he was concentrating on his work, as usual. Any time I emerged from my room he'd look startled—like he hadn't realized I was home—and then make a weird face that I think was supposed to be sympathetic.

The afternoon was a misery of nausea, sweating—more from the sweltering room than anything else—and damp, tangled sheets. I slept through suppertime, which was fine with me, and woke up later in the evening feeling a little better.

I moved around a bit, looking for a cooler spot in the bed, and saw that my iPod was next to me on the nightstand. When I powered it on there was a new message from Billy, which was kind of funny since I'd been thinking about him earlier. I figured he was trying to patch things up again but when I read it I got a bit of a shock.

Stop being such a jerk.

That sure made me mad. I made up my mind that I was definitely sticking to what I'd said the day he backed out on the trip. Most times when we fight and I say I'm not being friends anymore, I end up changing my mind after a few days, or sometimes even weeks. Longest was almost a month. Not this time. There are plenty of other guys I could hang around with.

I dozed off again a bit later and when I woke up the next morning I felt a lot better. It's amazing, how awful you can feel one day, and the next thing you know it's like there was never a thing wrong with you.

I made my way to the twins' cabin, glad to be outside and looking forward to a day doing something fun.

"Looking for the girls, are you?" their dad asked when he opened the door to my knock. His face was pale and it hit me that this was the first time I'd seen him without a smile. "I'm afraid they won't be out today, Adam. We're all sick—have been all night."

I said I'd had the same thing the day before and tried to cheer him with the news that it shouldn't last long, but I could see he wasn't in the mood to stand around chatting. I left and ambled down to the shore but after I'd kicked around a bit I was bored. I went back to our cabin.

Mom was washing dishes, singing to herself,

while dad tapped away at his laptop. He glanced up when he heard the screen door clatter behind me.

"Something wrong?"

"The twins are sick."

"You've really taken to them, haven't you?" he said with a big grin.

"There's no one else to hang around with." My face felt flushed all of a sudden. I hoped I wasn't getting sick again.

"You still collecting driftwood for Theo?" Dad asked. When I said I was, he closed his laptop, stood up, stretched, and picked up the car keys.

"What say we head into town, grab lunch somewhere, and then check out a stretch of shore you haven't already searched?"

"Sure!"

"June? Are you in?"

Mom tilted her head to the side and scrunched her mouth like she was thinking it over. She does that so you can see she's trying to make up her mind, but I'm pretty sure it's an act because she ends up saying, "no," every time she does that.

"You know what—I think I'll pass this time," she said. "You boys go ahead."

Just as I thought.

16

"It's great to see your mom happy with her work again, isn't it?" Dad said on the drive into town.

"Sure."

"Artists are sensitive in different ways from regular folk," he said. "Not in a bad way, mind you. It's just part of who they are."

"Was there a famous artist who cut off his ear once?" I asked, remembering something the twins had told me.

"That was van Gogh," Dad said. He glanced at me and gave my knee a quick slap. "But don't worry, your mother is too fond of her earrings to ever do that."

"Why did van Gogh do it?"

"He went off his head, I imagine," Dad said.

"Because he was sensitive?"

"No, no—that's not what I meant. With van Gogh,

it might have been from lead in the paint or something. I don't seem to know much about it really, but it's nothing to worry about. With your mother, I mean."

A couple of minutes passed before he spoke again. Then, he said, "We probably shouldn't mention this talk to your mom. She might not take it the right way."

In case you're wondering, I didn't think my mom was going to cut off her ear or anything that crazy, but she sure gets into strange moods at times. When that happens, she cries or hollers or goes to her room and slams the door shut for hardly any reason at all. I guess it's all part of being an artist, like my dad said.

We had burgers and milkshakes for lunch and then we made a quick stop at a Dollarama because Mom had asked Dad to pick up citronella candles to help keep the bugs away. After that we found a place to park near the river and walked along the shore looking for driftwood. Dad found a piece that looked pretty good, and then we backtracked to where the car was parked.

Back at Schooner Point, I saw that Mom was in the field with her easel set up again. I headed there to get another look at the painting she was working on and to tell her she missed out on a milkshake. Mom is a big fan of chocolate shakes.

The painting was almost finished and it was even better than I remembered. She was dabbing some grey into clouds and I stood there quietly in case she was concentrating.

"How'd you boys make out?" she asked as soon as she'd finished touching up the clouds. Her voice was happy and light.

"Good," I said. I decided not to mention the milkshakes after all. "We got a bunch of candles."

"Perfect," she said, dipping her brush in her water jar. "Any luck finding driftwood?"

I was telling her about the piece Dad found when a head appeared over the edge of the bank. It was Nevin, and he was carrying a canvas. He threw me a quick glare but as soon as he looked at my mom his face broke into a smile.

"I did what you said," he told her.

"And how did it go?"

"It felt a bit strange, but only at first," he said. "After that it was awesome."

Then he turned his canvas around for Mom to see what he'd painted. I don't know what *she* was expecting, but *I* thought it would be a scene from the shore, where he'd been painting. It wasn't.

"What is it?" I blurted.

"It's an abstract," Mom explained.

Nevin looked embarrassed. He started to turn the canvas away.

"It's *really* cool," I said. It was true—I liked it a lot. I stepped closer for a better look.

Nevin seemed suspicious but he stopped trying to hide the painting. Mom looked it over slowly, nodding and saying things about central colours and flow and other stuff that didn't mean a thing to me.

Nevin sure seemed to find Mom's comments interesting, judging by the expression on his face. He was hanging onto every word, asking questions and listening to her answers like she was giving him directions to buried treasure. But then *she* asked *him* a question.

"Are you planning to study art after you finish high school?"

All the light went out of Nevin's face. His head dropped and he mumbled, "My parents are against it. They don't think you can make a good living with art."

"There are a lot of misconceptions about that," Mom said. "Maybe your parents don't know all the careers an artist can have. You can do as well in some of them as in any other field."

"Really?" Nevin said.

"Absolutely. If they're against the idea, then it's up to you to learn what kind of jobs are possible and take that information to them. They're more likely to listen if you can prove what you're talking about."

"I will," Nevin promised. His smile was back.

"And if it doesn't change their mind—well then, you have to decide how much you want it. Lots of young people work part time and take student loans—if it matters enough, you'll find a way."

"If I have enough talent," he said.

"*I* think you do," I blurted, which made both of them turn and look at me in surprise.

Then Nevin laughed, and said, "That's encouraging, coming from someone who helped feed me a worm."

That got Mom's attention and I thought I'd be in trouble, but he laughed again and said, "It was nothing. Just an inside joke."

Nevin wasn't turning out to be so bad after all. In fact, the more I thought about it, he was like the opposite of the coyote in the story Theo had told. I had a feeling that the mean side of Nevin was an act and, for some reason, he was hiding a pretty okay guy underneath it.

The next morning he showed up at our door right after breakfast. He helped carry Mom's supplies and they headed off to the field to spend the morning painting.

Dad was back to work on his laptop so I headed over to cabin four, hoping for better news than I'd gotten the last time I was there. Mackenzie answered my knock.

"Are you better?" she asked before I could open my mouth.

"Me?"

"Yes. We went to get you the other day and your mom said you were awful sick."

"Oh, right." I'd almost forgotten my own day in bed. I told her I was fine and she told me she was fine, too, and then Makayla announced from behind her that she wouldn't mind being able to get out the door if Mackenzie could get her butt out of the way.

"Is that what I think it is?" Makayla asked as soon as we'd cleared out of her way.

I saw that she was staring at the piece of driftwood I'd brought along. "My dad found it yesterday," I said.

"Well, what are we waiting for?" Makayla practically yelled. "Let's go see Theo!"

I was a bit nervous about walking past Nevin with them but I didn't have anything to worry about. They marched by him with little more than a glance, and didn't even notice the slight nod he gave me. I thought he looked like he felt sorry for me, but I might have imagined that.

The girls talked so much on the way to Theo's that it's a wonder they had time to breathe. I guess they were making up for the quiet day they'd just had, but I could hardly keep up with what they were saying.

It was their usual recital of interesting facts. Stories and numbers and bits of trivia floated into the air and right by me as we walked along. The only thing I remembered by the end of it all was that most dust is actually dead skin cells that fall off people and their pets. That one was gross enough for me to want to remember to tell people back home. I was thinking I'd trick one of the guys into licking something dusty, and then let him know what he'd just eaten.

We got to Theo's place in no time, and before we knew it, he was holding the piece of driftwood and telling us all about it.

THE BAOBAB TREE

This limb is from a tree that is thousands of years old. It is known as the baobab, although some call it the boab tree. Surprisingly, in spite of its age, the tree from which this branch was taken is still alive. It can be found in Senegal, which is a country on the west coast of Northern Africa.

The baobab is unusual because its trunk can grow to be enormous. In time, it becomes hollow inside. Some baobab trees are even large enough to live in. This particular tree had not grown quite that big, although its trunk was very large compared to trees we see around here.

On the beautiful coast of Senegal, there was a peaceful village where everybody lived in harmony. You could often hear the people of the village singing as they went about their work. Even though they did not have much, they were content with what they did have, and for this reason they were happy.

In this village lived a girl who was called Binata. Binata was fourteen years old and the daughter of a fisherman. She was a lovely girl, slim and graceful, with skin like polished ebony and eyes as dark as a moonless night.

Each day, Binata would spend the morning helping her mother. After that she would make her way through the village to the water's edge, waiting for the fishermen to come with their catch. As her bare feet padded softly on the dusty ground, villagers would call out greetings, which she answered with good cheer and a smile.

Often, Binata would fish at the water's edge as she watched for the boats. As she did so, she sang a song,

Come fish, flick your tail
Come to the land
Come with your rainbow scale
Come to my hand.

Later, the fishermen and some of the village women worked together, gutting and cleaning the day's catch. The days passed simply and happily for Binata and her village. But that was all about to change.

The change came because the rain stopped falling on the land to the east. This brought a drought to villages that were only two days' walk from Binata's beautiful coastal home. In the place without rain, there was not enough water. There was not enough food. People began to die. At first, it was the sickly and feeble, but they knew it was only a matter of time before the healthy would follow. Fear gripped the hearts of the people in those other villages. They watched the sky and prayed for clouds but day after day the sky was blue and clear, and the blazing sun mocked their growing thirst.

The people in those villages gathered around their leaders demanding that something be done. *If you do not act, we will all die*, they said with one voice. The land they possessed had turned against them. And so, a plan was formed. They must seek a new place to live.

Scouts were sent out to help the leaders choose the right path. They returned with news that there was a large and prosperous town that could be reached on foot in several days. This town, they reported, was too strong for them to overtake, but south of that town was a village that would be easy for their warriors to defeat.

And so it was. This was how it came to pass that Binata's happy village became enslaved. They were forced to give their homes and all that they possessed to strangers. Each day when the fishermen returned with their catch, they had to watch with empty bellies as the intruders satisfied their hunger. The villagers had to make do with the scraps that were left over.

Things went on this way for some time. Then,

one morning, Binata's father and two other men from her village managed to slip away and go to the larger town to the north of their village. There, they asked what it would cost to hire the town's warriors to help them. It was with heavy hearts that they returned with the news that the amount was much greater than the village could possibly pay. The situation seemed hopeless.

One day, Binata was at her usual place, fishing while she waited for the boats. As she lifted one fish from the water, she was startled to hear it speak.

"Wait, friend!" the fish said.

"You are no friend to me," Binata answered.

"Let me go," said the fish, "and I will prove it."

"I cannot let you go," Binata answered. "There is little enough food to feed the waiting mouths." She raised her knife.

"Wait!" cried the fish. "If you let me go, I will make you wealthy."

Binata smiled to herself. She knew that talking fish could be very tricky. Still, it would be interesting to hear what this fish had to say.

"Not so very far from here is a sunken ship," the fish told her. "In that ship, there are trunks filled with gold pieces. Let me go, and I will bring you a piece of gold every day until you have everything that your heart desires."

Binata laughed. "You are a sly one," she said. Again she made ready to put her knife to the fish but something stopped her.

"That is the first time I have laughed since the intruders came," she said. "And for that, you shall have your freedom."

With that, she leaned forward and let the fish slip away into the cool, blue water.

But the fish had not tricked Binata. The very next day it was there, waiting in the shallow water. It caught her eye with a flick of its tail and when she reached down, it spit a gold piece into her hand.

Binata hid the gold piece in the folds of her garment but she knew she must find a safer place. If the intruders discovered it, they would take it from her. Binata's eyes swept the land around her and settled on an old baobab tree. It had been there for hundreds of years, and its fat trunk had grown hollow. Binata hurried to the tree and slipped her hand into an opening near the bottom. She reached back as far as she could and dropped the gold piece.

Each day the fish returned with more gold and each day Binata made another deposit into the baobab's trunk. This continued for weeks, and finally there was enough. Binata told her father of the hidden treasure, and once again a party was sent to the northern town. This time, they were able to meet the warriors' price and, with their help, the intruders were easily driven off.

Happiness and harmony were restored to the village. And Binata never saw the fish again.

I was starting to notice that Theo's driftwood stories ended before you wanted them to. Every one of them left me wondering things, and there was no way to get answers.

That's what was going through my head when Mackenzie said, "Imagine if Binata hadn't let the fish go!"

"Their village would never have been freed," Makayla said.

"And she didn't even think the fish was telling the truth," Mackenzie said with a faraway look on her face. "She must have been so surprised when it showed up the next day."

"I wonder why the fish stopped coming," Makayla said. "Binata could have been rich!"

"That's right!" Makenzie said. "Didn't he promise her she would have everything she wanted, Theo?"

"Yes," Theo said. "That was his promise."

"Then why didn't he keep it?" I asked.

"But he did." Theo said. He smiled, but it was a serious smile so we knew he wasn't kidding. There was quiet for a few minutes, while we thought about what he meant.

It was Theo who broke the silence. "Would anyone like a bird's nest cookie?"

A cookie made out of a bird's nest didn't sound too appealing to me. Of course, I knew that Theo's snacks were hardly ever what you expected them to be. So I said I'd try one. And the girls both said, "Yes," right away.

Let me tell you, when I sank my teeth into that cookie I was sure glad I hadn't turned it down. It was the best cookie I'd ever had, covered in coconut, with raspberry filling in a dent in the centre of it. It didn't take me long to reach out when Theo passed the plate around a second time.

"It does me good to have youngsters dropping by," Theo said.

"And we love coming here," Makayla told him.

"But this will be our last visit," Mackenzie added. "We're going home tomorrow."

"I thought you were staying for two weeks," I said.

"We *did*, silly," said Makayla.

"Don't you mean *sweetie*?" Mackenzie asked. They both giggled.

I could hardly believe that two weeks had gone by already. Making new friends like Joey and the twins was great, but then having them leave and not knowing if I'd ever see them again wasn't so hot.

That night I had a dream. When it started, I was walking on the shore with the girls and Joey. We were on our way to Theo's place but after we'd gone a short distance, I spotted something on the ground and stopped to investigate. It seemed to be a piece of driftwood, but when I got closer, I saw instead that it was a large fish. I looked around to tell the others, but they had vanished. That was when the fish gasped and spoke.

"Help me back into the water, friend," it cried.

I knelt and was startled to see that the fish had Billy's face. But when I reached my hand out to help it, I discovered that my arm was covered in grey hair. Fear raced through my veins as I understood what this meant.

I was the coyote.

I jolted awake and lay there with my heart thumping in my chest. It slowed to normal after a few minutes, but my thoughts didn't settle so quickly. By the time I'd sorted through them I knew what I had to do.

Sliding out of bed, I tiptoed to the other room, where I'd left my iPod. There was a message I needed to send.

When I got up the next morning I was glad

to see that cabin four wasn't empty yet. When Joey's family left so early it had felt strange that I never had a chance to say goodbye. At least I'd be able to do that with Mackenzie and Makayla.

They were all taking things out to the car when I got there so I pitched in and helped. Then I noticed that Nevin and his folks had just finished packing their car too. I ran over as Nevin was about to get into the back seat. He was back to wearing his sullen face and I was glad I had seen the other side of him.

"I have to tell you something," I said.

He looked about as interested as a rock.

"You never ate a worm," I said. "It was a trick. The piece you saw was rubber."

For a second I saw anger flare in his eyes. He looked across at the twins, who were standing, staring at me. Then he relaxed and kind of grinned a bit. He said, "Good enough then," and gave me a feeble punch on the shoulder.

"What was that about?" Mackenzie asked when I got back to their place.

"Just something between guys," I said.

She looked annoyed but she didn't pester me about it, and when they were ready to leave she surprised me with a quick hug.

I watched their car drive off and wondered if the next batch of campers would bring anyone interesting. With nothing else to do, I made up my mind to hang around and see.

It didn't look too promising. I spent part of the morning and most of the afternoon watching. Not all of the cabins got new people—there were two besides ours whose campers were staying on. One was a young couple that seemed to divide their time evenly between arguing and making up. The other was a pair of old ladies who were sisters. Mom said they were spinsters. That's what my Great-aunt Marilyn is too, so I knew it meant they'd never gotten married.

It seemed that mostly everyone who came to Schooner Point was friendly, but it was still going to be boring if none of the new batch of renters had kids. My age, that is. Two of the cabins that filled up the day after the twins left were couples with toddlers.

I don't care for little kids. They're always wailing or yelling about something or other. When they run, they never look where they're going. Instead, they turn their heads and look sideways—and *keep* looking sideways until they bang into something. But if one of them crashes into you and falls over, it's somehow your fault. And, their noses seem to run about eighty percent of the time, which is gross.

At supper, Mom commented that if there was no one my age around this week, I might be able to make a few bucks doing some babysitting. "You're almost old enough, and I'm sure it would be fine, since your father and I are right here," she said. Then she gave me one of her '*great idea, huh?*' smiles.

I don't think the look I gave back left her with any doubts about what I thought of that plan.

"The boy looks like he's been sucking on a lemon, June," Dad said.

Mom shrugged. "It was just a thought."

I hoped that was the end of it. Mom has been known to bring something up again after you thought it was settled. She tries to sneak it in front of you in a new way, like you won't notice it's a recycled idea.

Dad and I did the dishes after supper and then I wandered down to the shore. By now, it felt familiar, like it was a part of my world. I skipped a few stones out into the water and kept my eyes open for any new driftwood that might have come in on the tide, but there was nothing. I sat on a big stone and watched the waves lap the shore for a while. If you've ever spent time staring out at a river or lake, you probably know how peaceful that made me feel.

A cool breeze came up after a bit and I decided to go back to the cabin to see if my dad was done with his laptop. I'd been meaning to check on Facebook for Joey, and I thought I might as well look for the twins while I was at it—just for something to do. I never had a chance though, because Mom and Dad decided it was board-game night. We played Clue and Monopoly and by then I was ready for bed.

I checked my iPod before I turned in for the night. There were no messages.

First thing I noticed when I went outside the next morning was that there was a van pulled up in front of the only cabin that had still been empty the day before. I walked over, thinking there might be kids my age, but that hope disappeared when an old couple came out onto the deck.

I was about to turn around when the woman spied me and yelled, "Hello, youngster!"

I said, "Hello," back and then stood there feeling foolish.

"Lookit here, Mack," she said, tapping on the old guy's arm with the back of her fingers. "This young lad appears to be about Ethan's age."

Mack squinted in my direction and made a grunting sound that could have meant anything.

"Speak up, then! How old are you?" the woman asked.

"Almost twelve," I said.

"Do you mean you're eleven?" she said.

I agreed that was the case.

"If you're eleven, just say so. Don't be wishing your life away by adding on numbers."

"Yes, ma'am."

"Ethan just turned twelve," she told me.

"I don't know who Ethan is," I pointed out.

"Well, hold onto your hat and I'll introduce you," she said. "Land sakes, young people these days are impatient." She turned toward the doorway and hollered, "Ethan! There's someone here that wants to meet you."

A blond kid appeared in the doorway, peered at me for a second, and then came out. Older or not, he was a bit shorter than me.

"Ethan, this here is—" The woman's voice trailed off for a second and then she let out a sound that was a sort of cross between a laugh and a bark. "Look at me, I didn't even ask your name. What is it?"

"Adam," I said, and she restarted her introduction.

"Ethan, this is Martin. He's eleven and he's camping here too. Or, I think he is anyway. Are you staying here with your folks, Martin?"

"It's *Adam*," I said. "And yes, we're here until the end of August."

Ethan came across the deck and down the two steps. "I'll be back in a few minutes, Gram," he said. "I gotta ask Adam about a couple of things."

He walked past me with hardly a glance. It seemed, from what he'd told his grandmother, that I was supposed to go with him so I fell into step and followed him through the centre of the park. When he reached the edge of the woods he just kept walking, but he stopped after a minute and plunked down on a fallen tree. I plunked down too.

"So, you're here for the month, are you?" he asked.

"Yeah. We've been here since the start of July," I said.

He whistled. It was a long, mournful sound and I couldn't help feeling a bit envious. I've never been any good at whistling.

"You must've been bored outta your skull," Ethan said. "Lucky for you, that's about to change now that I'm here."

"It hasn't been that bad," I said. I wasn't sure why I didn't come right out and tell him I'd been having a great time. But I was interested in what he had in mind. There was something about him—the way he walked with a sort of swagger, and talked as if he was in charge. Not that I meant to let him boss me around.

"You don't have to pretend around me," Ethan said. "This isn't my first time around the block."

"You've been here before?"

"Not this exact place. But I go somewhere like this with my grandparents for a month every summer."

"It isn't so bad here," I said. Actually, I thought it was one of the nicest places I'd ever spent my vacation but I somehow couldn't say so to Ethan.

"Don't get me wrong, Adam. Camping is great if you like being bored. But I gotta tell you, I'm the kind of guy who needs excitement. I hope you're not against having fun."

"Of course I'm not," I said.

"All right, then. In that case, I guess you can hang around with me. Just so long as you don't start acting like a girl."

"Don't worry about *that*," I said. At the same time, I couldn't help wondering what Ethan would have thought of Mackenzie and Makayla. I bet they could have changed his mind about girls pretty quick.

"Okay, then," Ethan said. He stood up and slapped himself in the stomach. "Gramps put a batch of biscuits in the oven just before you landed. They should be ready right about now."

"Your *grandfather* makes biscuits?" I asked. My grandfather likes to say that he and my grandmother are a perfect team—she likes to cook and he likes to eat.

"Gramps worked as a baker his whole life," Ethan said. "You saying there's something wrong with that?"

"That's not what I meant," I said. "I was just wondering."

We walked the short distance back to the cluster

of cabins but when I started to turn off at mine, Ethan stopped in his tracks and stared at me like I was crazy.

"*Where* you going?" he asked. "We've gotta get to those biscuits while they're still warm."

Since he hadn't invited me, I didn't quite see why he seemed so put out. Either way, I was glad to go along with him. The smell of the biscuits met us when we went through the door and, beside them on the table, were bowls of mashed strawberries and whipped cream.

"You're just in time, boys," Ethan's gram said. She was already spooning berries onto a biscuit, which she'd split across the middle and opened onto a plate. She added a big dollop of cream on top of it and passed me the plate and a spoon.

"You're not lactose intolerant, are you, Martin?" she asked. "I should have asked before I put that whipping cream on. Seems nowadays every second kid you run into has some kind of digestion problem."

"Thanks—and I'm fine," I said. "But my name isn't Martin, it's Adam."

"You're welcome," she said. "Ethan, get a couple of mugs for you and Martin. If he drinks tea, that is. Do you drink tea, Martin?"

"Sure he does," Ethan said. He grinned at me. "Don't feel too bad about the name," he said in an undertone. "Once Gram gets mixed up, that's it. Believe it or not, my name is actually Paul."

"Seriously?"

He answered that by bursting out laughing. Wise guy. But I got over being annoyed as soon as I took the first bite of biscuit and berries. It was right up there as one of the best things I'd ever eaten. I suddenly understood why Ethan had been in such a hurry to get back to his place while they were warm.

We each had another one and drank our tea. I had mine with two spoons of sugar and enough milk to make it pale, and it was perfect. After that, Gram told us she was going to have to put the run to us while she finished getting things organized.

I kept waiting for Ethan to reveal his big plans for excitement, but we mostly spent the day wandering around aimlessly. I figured he was probably one of those guys who goes around talking big but never really doing anything. Boy, was I wrong.

20

Ethan showed up at my cabin the next morning just as I was chewing my last bite of toast. Mom and Dad hadn't met him yet, so they put him through the usual introductions and then let him in. He sauntered over to the table and looked at me like I was an alien.

"You're not even dressed yet," he said.

"That will only take me a couple of minutes," I told him.

"Don't forget to brush your teeth," Mom said as I headed toward my bedroom.

"I know that, Mom," I grumbled. I hurried into my clothes and brushed my teeth, hoping Mom wouldn't pick today for what she calls a 'spot check' to make sure I've done a good job. I could picture the smirk on Ethan's face if he got to witness something like that.

Luckily, she didn't, and we were out the door and on our way. We walked down the road the opposite way we'd gone the day before, because Ethan said he wanted to scope out the place a bit more, whatever that meant. After we'd passed a bunch of houses he turned to me and asked, "So, this is seriously all there is around here? Just a bunch of houses and stuff?"

"Pretty much," I agreed.

"Might as well head back, then," he said. "This was a waste of time."

We went back as far as the cabins and then crossed the field and made our way down to the shore. I went ahead and told Ethan about Theo, even though I was a bit worried he'd find that boring, like everything else.

"Theo can tell really cool things about where a piece of driftwood is from just by holding it in his hands," I said.

"Yeah, *sure* he can," Ethan scoffed.

That made me mad. "I guess you think you know everything," I said.

Ethan's head turned and he gave me a look, but it wasn't what I was expecting. He seemed, I don't know, kind of *interested*, like he'd just come across some new bug he'd never seen before.

"I wish I hadn't forgot to bring my cell phone," he said. "If I had it, I'd call my dad and ask him if he thinks that could be true."

"How would your dad know?" I asked.

"He's a scientist. An *important* one. So's my mom. Why do you think I have to go places with my grandparents in the summer? Because that's when my mom and dad travel all over the world doing research and stuff, that's why."

"Where are they now?" I asked.

"It's hard to say. They go wherever their research takes them. Could be Iceland or Brazil or pretty near anywhere."

"My mom's a painter," I said, but that didn't impress him like it had the twins.

"That's why she's not travelling all over the place doing important research like my folks," he said. "Anyway, I think my dad could straighten you out about this Theo guy. If I had my phone that is."

"Theo's nice," I said.

"Nice, schmice," Ethan answered. "That doesn't mean he's not making up the stuff he tells you."

"It sounds real," I said.

"I'll just have to go hear one for myself," Ethan said. "How far away does he live?"

"It's a bit of a walk down the shore," I said. "But we'd have to find a piece of driftwood before we went. Sometimes that takes a while, especially since I've been checking the shore around here pretty regular."

"Why kill ourselves scrounging for one?" Ethan said. "I saw some driftwood when we were kicking around yesterday. When I check a place out, I take it all in. It's probably in my blood. Come on."

Curious, I followed him along the bank. We could see the backs of the houses we'd passed the day before, and I noticed he was peering through the trees at them. Suddenly, he stopped and pointed.

"There!" he said. Then he turned and put a finger to his lips. "Keep quiet while I go get one."

I stood there, still confused, as Ethan crept toward one of the houses. He crouched a bit and looked around as he moved closer and closer. That was when I saw it—a flower garden at the side of the deck. There were stones around the edge of the garden and four or five pieces of driftwood arranged among purple and yellow flowers.

I wanted to yell at him to forget it, that he couldn't go around stealing things, but my voice seemed frozen. I took a step or two toward him but by then he'd snatched the closest piece and was hurrying back toward me.

"Come on!" he said as he zipped past and disappeared down over the bank.

With my heart pounding as hard as it would have if I'd stolen it myself, I raced down the bank and caught up with him on the shore. He was clutching the wood, bent over and panting, but when he got a glimpse of my face he burst out laughing.

"Don't tell me you're going to weird out over an old hunk of branch," he said.

"It belonged to the people in that house."

"It's not like I stole their car," Ethan said, still grinning. "I thought you were up for some excitement. I guess you were lying about that."

"Was not," I said.

"Well, then, quit going on about a worthless old chunk of tree. Now, where's this guy's place? I can't wait to hear his fairy tale."

I suddenly wasn't the least bit keen about taking Ethan to Theo's place. "Not if you're going to be rude or make fun of his story," I said.

"Calm down," Ethan told me. "What do you think, I'm that big a jerk that I'm going to be mean to an old guy?"

I gave him what I hoped was a menacing look as a final warning, and started off toward Theo's place. One thing I was glad about was that Theo knew he didn't have to pay anything anymore. Without even thinking it over I knew that Ethan would have taken the money—for a stolen piece of wood. I couldn't even imagine how mad that would have made me.

Usually, it seems like a long walk to Theo's place, so I was surprised how fast we got there. I saw him as soon as our heads cleared the top of the bank, sitting in his usual spot on the back deck.

"Hi Theo," I called. "It's me, Adam."

"Adam—hello!" he answered. "Come right along."

"This is Ethan," I said as we reached the deck.

"He's here camping with his grandparents."

"Pleased to meet you, Ethan," Theo said. He stuck his hand forward and Ethan shook it and said he was pleased to meet Theo too. So far so good.

"I brought a piece of driftwood for you," Ethan said, putting it into Theo's hands. "Adam says you collect it."

"That I do," Theo agreed. His fingers moved over the wood, pressing, tapping gently, gliding along as he drifted with it, into its past.

When he spoke, it seemed I could hear the whisper of waves in his voice.

THE MOUNTAIN ASH

This fine specimen comes from a tree called *Eucalyptus regnans*, better known as the mountain ash of Australia. This particular mountain ash was no ordinary tree. Many years ago it was the tallest tree in the world, even surpassing the glorious height of the magnificent California redwood, although the redwood is normally the tallest of all trees.

This bit of limb was part of a tree that once lived in the province of Tasmania. Tasmania is part of Australia, but it is not on the mainland. It is an island near the south-eastern part of Australia. There are many beautiful places on our planet, and Tasmania is certainly one of them.

When the moon was full and round, and it rose over the land, this tree seemed like a hand, reaching up to wave hello. The aborigine people who lived nearby used the tree as a meeting place and called it the Cloud Tree because of the way it stretched up into the sky.

The Cloud Tree was part of the local lore, and there were several stories about why it had grown so tall—more than forty feet higher than other mountain ash.

One such story told of how a maiden had wept beside the tree when her betrothed was missing at sea. Her tears were so pure and full of love that it had caused a great growth spurt. The tree grew so tall that one day, when the sun's angle was just right, it cast a shadow over the waves, and that shadow reached all the way to her sweetheart's boat. He was able to follow it and make his way home at last.

Another story told of a mother who watched daily from the treetop for her son's boat to return from a long journey. As the days passed, her worry grew and one day she placed a spell on the tree, so it would grow taller and taller, allowing her to see further. The spell worked, but the son's boat never returned. One day, the heartbroken woman climbed the tree with her very last breath of hope, and disappeared forever into its branches.

These and other stories were told again and again over the years, but there was only one person on the whole island who knew the truth. Her name was Toora, and she was The Keeper of Secrets. Toora knew that the tree had not grown from a maiden's tears or a mother's spell. It grew because the heartbeat of the people joined the earth and sun in the soil of that one, special place. It grew with a purpose, and that purpose was to tell the world that this was a place like no other.

Toora kept her secrets wisely. Because everyone knew that she was The Keeper of Secrets, it was not unusual for those around her to try to find out some of the things she knew. They would pester, flatter, and even try to trick her into telling, but she kept her own counsel. Toora remembered the words of her beloved grandfather, who had passed the role down to her.

"Watch the eyes of those who come with questions," he told her. "The eyes will tell you if the question is asked for good."

"How will the eyes tell me this, Grandfather?" Toora had asked.

"You will see a light shining in the eyes of those who seek answers. Red means the information they seek will be used in anger, green tells you the question comes from envy, deep violet rises from pride and golden yellow from greed."

"And the light that comes from good?" Toora had wanted to know.

"Look for light that is transparent. It has nothing to hide," Grandfather had told her.

Toora had been wise in her duties as The Keeper of Secrets, but she knew her days were coming to a close. It was time to pass her knowledge to a new generation. Toora had given much thought to whom she should choose for this role. At last, she settled on her great-niece, Kiah.

Kiah was a quiet, solitary child. When Toora sent for her, she went obediently and listened solemnly as her great-aunt told her that she was to become The Keeper of Secrets. Her training began immediately and continued for two years, until Toora passed away.

At that time, the people of the island held a great feast to bid farewell to Toora and to welcome Kiah to her new role. Kiah's heart was warm and happy as good wishes flowed to her ears. Before long, she overcame her shyness and began to enjoy her new popularity.

In short order, Kiah found herself surrounded by people who wanted to know the secrets she held. She quickly learned that their smiles faded and they turned from her when she did not tell them what they wanted to know. Even so, she was determined to keep the secrets safe, and to share them only with the worthy, as she had been taught.

But it was not very long until Kiah realized that many of her newfound friends were slipping away. She remembered how lonely life had been when she had spent so much time on her own. The thought of returning to a solitary lifestyle caused her sorrow. And then, Kiah had an idea.

What if she gave answers without actually

divulging the secrets that had been entrusted to her? Would it be so wrong to make up answers to satisfy the ears of those asking questions? In this way, she would continue to be surrounded by attention and friends.

And so it went. Kiah gave advice and made up lavish stories. One day she might tell a farmer to plant his crops the next time he saw an echidna at an anthill. Another day she may offer a simple stone as a talisman, or tell a young woman to accept a suitor's hand if a lone cloud graced the sky on the third day after his proposal.

Kiah did not see that her advice was often wrong or that it sometimes caused harm. Rather, she became convinced that she had a special gift of wisdom and that the advice she dispensed had value. But those around her were beginning to grumble. They were questioning her words and asking each other if there was some mistake. The Keeper of Secrets seemed to be giving information that was not true. And before long, they understood. Kiah was entertaining herself at their expense—telling lies and giving worthless advice.

Even so, they were cautious about voicing their suspicions. Toora had named Kiah as her successor, and Toora had been respected and true. In short order, they turned the tables on Kiah without her knowing it. They amused themselves by pretending to seek her knowledge, but they mocked her behind her back.

And then came the day when one of the island's most powerful men decided that he would build a new home, and the place that pleased him for this purpose was the very place where the great mountain ash known as The Cloud Tree stood.

It was the man's eldest son who sought Kiah's advice on the matter. As he formed his question, Kiah was preparing an answer in her usual fashion, but in the last second, she saw that the light in his eyes was transparent. The importance of the moment made her heart pound. At last the time had come for her to share a real secret.

"You must tell your father that he cannot build in that place," she said solemnly. "The tree that stands above others is the tallest tree in the world. Someday, our island will be known near and wide for this wonder."

The young man thanked her for her words and went on his way. When he shared the story with his friends there was much laughing and merriment. The tallest tree in the world indeed! No one took the warning seriously. No one even considered that this time, Kiah's words may be true.

That is why the great tree was felled, and lives no more.

And this limb alone, remains.

As Theo finished speaking I glanced over at Ethan. I could see that he'd been drawn into the story but I also saw that he was determined not to believe it. He met my glance with a mocking smile forming on his lips. I hoped with all my might that he would keep his word and not say anything mean or rude.

It was Theo who broke into those thoughts. He stood and put the piece of driftwood on his chair. "Boys, you'd be doing me a favour if you'd have a scratch-me-back. I'm going to be away for a bit and I'm afraid they'll be ruined by the time I get back.

"Are you going for your surgery?" I asked, excited.

"If my nerves don't give out," he chuckled. "My daughter is coming soon, to take me to the hospital, and I'll be spending a week or two at her home afterward. So how about those scratch-me-backs?"

I said, "Sure," and Ethan said, "Yes, please, Theo," as if he was the most polite kid in the world. A few minutes later we were munching on thin, flat cookies that didn't look like much but sure tasted great. I had three, to help Theo out, and Ethan gobbled down four.

We'd just finished our snack when the crunch of gravel under a car's tires in the driveway let us all know that Theo's daughter had arrived. She came out to where we were sitting and told Theo that she was going to tidy up a bit and then they'd be on their way.

"I'd best go in and make sure she doesn't give the place a complete overhaul," Theo said. "She's a great one for organizing—I can hardly find anything after she's done."

We got up to leave and I told Theo good luck and said I'd see him when he got back.

"And I'll see you, Adam," he said. "It'll be the first time."

"I'll still be here, too," Ethan said. He seemed a bit sulky for some reason.

"I'll be glad to have you *both* come visit again," Theo said. "Oh, and before you go—there's one more thing I wanted to tell you about this piece of driftwood."

He picked it up and held it while he spoke.

"Tasmania was its first home, all right, but it wasn't the last one. After it made its journey here to Canada, it found a new home. I'm not sure exactly where, but it lived among stones and flowers, and I believe that's the place it was meant to be. So, if you boys wouldn't mind obliging an old feller, I'd like you to take it there now."

With that, Theo passed the piece of wood over to Ethan, gave us a wave, and disappeared inside his house. Let me tell you, the look on Ethan's face was something to see. There wasn't so much as a trace of the smug expression he usually had on.

Ethan never said a single word the whole way back. When we reached the bank by the house he'd taken the driftwood from, he scooted up the hill, walked across to the garden, and put it back in place without the slightest hesitation.

I think he was waiting for me to say "I told you so," or something. I might have been tempted if he hadn't looked like he was in shock. And, I guess I should admit I was surprised myself.

It wasn't until we got to the field across from our cabins that Ethan spoke up.

"There's got to be an explanation," he said.

"Like what?"

"I don't know. Maybe he's friends with the people who had it in their garden, and he recognized it."

"But he can't see."

"Maybe he recognized it by feel," Ethan said. "He probably goes around mauling everybody's driftwood, since he likes it so much." He didn't even sound like he believed that himself. I guess it wasn't impossible, but it sure didn't seem likely to me.

Ethan didn't seem to want to talk about it any more. "I'm starved," he said, even though he'd just eaten four of Theo's scratch-me-backs.

We headed across the road toward his cabin but before we got there we found his grandparents sitting at one of the community picnic tables. There was an assortment of things spread out on it and when she spied us, Ethan's gram called out, "Over here boys!" like we might have just walked right past without noticing them.

"I thought you two might be along," she said as we sat down at the table. "So I brought out extras of everything."

"Boys get hungry," added Gramps. He was buttering a biscuit from the day before.

"Guess what I made to drink!" Gram said.

"Lemonade," Ethan said. He jabbed me with his elbow and jerked his head toward the glass pitcher that sat in the middle of the table. There were a bunch of lemons, cut in half and floating around in there. It would have been hard to get it wrong.

"That's right!" Gram said. "I know how much you like my fresh-squeezed lemonade. Your father was crazy about it too, when he was little."

"I don't suppose anyone's squeezing him fresh lemonade where he is now," Gramps said.

"Hey! There's a guy near here who tells great

stories about driftwood," Ethan announced. "You can't meet him for a while, though. He's going to get an operation on his eyes."

Gram asked some questions about Theo as she dug out plastic cups and poured lemonade into them. She passed me mine first but when she reached by me to give Ethan his, her arm knocked my cup over. It ran through the spaces in the picnic table and soaked my pants and shoes.

"Wouldn't that just rot your socks!" Gram said. "I'm awfully sorry, Martin."

"No sense crying over spilled milk," Gramps said. "Or lemonade—right boys?"

"You just whip those wet duds off and I'll take them back to the cabin and have them good as new in a jig," Gram said.

That's when I said I *really* had to get home. I did too. I was sure there'd be a message for me by now and I was anxious to check.

But there was nothing.

23

Ethan was a lot of fun to hang around with, although sometimes his bossiness kind of got to me. I'd thought Joey was bossy, but he was nothing next to this guy. I mostly tried to ignore that part of him, though, because he wasn't lying when he'd told me he liked excitement. We did a lot of spying over the next few weeks. It might sound boring when I explain what we did, but it really wasn't.

We figured out a bunch of places where we could watch a few houses at the same time, and then we'd lay low and wait for someone to come outside. Sometimes whoever it was would get in a car and drive off, which was useless to us. But lots of times they'd be doing things around their yards—taking care of gardens and lawns, playing with pets, washing cars, reading, sunbathing, puttering around in out-buildings—the list just went on and on.

As soon as we had a "target" as Ethan insisted we call them, we'd inch closer, bit by bit. We'd crawl on our stomachs through long grass or sneak up behind trees. When we got close enough, we'd try to get them to look away from where we were hiding by tossing pebbles or small sticks in the opposite direction. Then we'd see if we could make a dash for cover and get even closer.

We nearly always got caught. Well, not caught, but spotted. Then we'd turn and hightail it like a couple of scared rabbits, racing away and dropping out of sight. It was so much fun, which made it hard not to laugh out loud and give away our hiding spots—not that anyone ever actually came after us.

Once in a while we managed to go undetected, even when we got really close to our target. When that happened, we'd stay still and watch for a few minutes. Unfortunately, no one ever did anything too interesting, so we'd end up slinking off and looking for something else to do.

When we were just kicking around the shore, Ethan talked a lot about his folks. I could see why he liked excitement so much. His mom and dad did amazing things. They spent days in the deepest, darkest caves in the world, collecting specimens for their research. They climbed mountains and hiked across deserts where you'd see nothing but sand for weeks on end. They survived grave dangers in South American jungles. And Ethan had lost track of how many times they'd parachuted into the middle of nowhere.

There seemed to be no end to the places they went or the dangers they encountered. But the main thing he talked about was how, in a few more years, he was going to start going along on the research trips.

"Won't you be scared?" I asked.

"Me? Scared?" Ethan laughed good and hard about that, but I wasn't totally convinced. I don't know how a guy could have poisonous snakes slithering around his neck, or deadly spiders running all over his arms and legs, and not be scared. That was the kind of thing that happened to his parents all the time.

"I feel sorry for you, Adam," Ethan told me one day. "I mean, not to insult your mom—I guess her paintings are okay. And your dad, what does he do all day? Boring computer stuff. They're not exactly getting you ready for a life of thrills."

I didn't like that talk much, but it was hard to argue with what he was saying. My dad's job *was* boring. As for Mom, ever since she'd had that conversation with the twins, there'd been a change in her. She was happier—humming and smiling, and more like her old self, and her paintings had gotten a lot better than just "okay." Still, I know her work isn't what you could call thrilling—not the way Ethan meant. So, I was a little embarrassed. It was hard not to be when I compared my parents with Ethan's.

It was tempting to point out that his grandparents weren't exactly entertaining either. I stopped myself because they'd been real nice to me, except for Ethan's Gram calling me Martin all the time. And anyway, it was worth putting up with Ethan's bragging if it meant having someone to hang around with.

We ate lunch with Ethan's Gram and Gramps most days. My mom kept saying we should even things out a bit more but it was hard to get ahead of Gram when it came to meals. A couple of times, Mom walked over right after breakfast, to tell Gram she'd be happy to make lunch for us, only to find Gram had made a chowder or a pasta salad the night before.

"They probably enjoy having the kids around, June," Dad told her. "And it gives them something to do."

Something to do was never a problem for Gram as far as I could tell. She was always busy, cooking and knitting and sewing, and saying things like, "Land sakes, if I drop another stitch this sweater's going to have two neck holes," and "Wouldn't that just frost your gizzard," anytime she made a mistake. Gram made a lot of mistakes, and she had no trouble identifying the problem each time. It would be a faulty recipe, print that was too fine, instructions a Rhodes Scholar couldn't follow—anything and everything except Gram.

Gramps did the baking. Lots of it. He made so many breads and cookies and squares that Ethan suggested we could set up a baked goods stand and sell some. Gramps said he couldn't go for that idea, and then he came up with a different plan. The next thing we knew, we were going around to the other cabins giving stuff away. "Share the wealth," Gramps said. No one complained about that except Ethan.

We explored the shore in both directions, looking for anything interesting. One day we found a great piece of driftwood tangled in some old weeds. After that, we checked every so often to see if Theo was back, but he must have been having a good time at his daughter's place because his house was still closed up and quiet.

All in all, everything went along smoothly for the first half of August. And then Ethan decided we were going to steal a boat.

24

I'm not saying I wasn't part of it. I was. Never mind that it took Ethan four days of nagging and persuading and calling me a girl. I could have kept right on saying "no" if I'd been a bit stronger. And if I'm telling the whole truth, you might as well know that there was a little part of me that wanted to do it. I guess you could say that I let myself be talked into it.

"You're looking at this whole thing all wrong," Ethan said. "It's not really stealing unless we're going to keep it. Which we're not."

"It's stealing if you take it without asking," I said.

"Think of it this way: it's just like that piece of driftwood we borrowed," he said, conveniently forgetting that wasn't quite accurate. "All we're going to do is move the boat a little ways. When we're done, we'll put it back where it was. No one will even know it was touched."

I thought about that for a minute.

"Besides, you can tell that nobody has used it for years," Ethan added. "We could probably keep it and it wouldn't even be missed."

"No way!" I said.

"Okay, so we borrow it for a couple of hours. One time. What's the big deal?"

Bit by bit, I weakened, and the more I did, the stronger and more insistent Ethan got. And then I said it.

"Okay."

His eyes lit up. "All right!" he said. "I knew you had it in you!"

"But just *one* time," I said. "I mean it."

"Sure, no problem. That's all I want."

Now that it was decided, I let myself feel the excitement. It was even better than spying. We made our way to the older home where we'd seen the boat. Near the house were a number of outbuildings, grey and weathered. We'd made the discovery four days earlier behind a large shed.

It was a small boat, turned upside down and leaning against the back wall of the shed. We flipped it over without much difficulty and discovered a couple of wooden paddles tucked under the seats inside it.

It slid easily along the tall grass so it didn't take us long to drag it to a field that was out of sight of the house. Then we got in and pretended to paddle and said all the seafaring things we could think of, like, "Ahoy," and "Avast, matey," and "Land Ho!" We sentenced a few scallywags to walk the plank but relented at the last minute and let them swab the deck instead.

It was cool sitting in it, hidden from view. We'd agreed on a few hours but it was longer than that before we finally decided it was time to take it back. Once it was in the same spot where we'd gotten it, we headed to Ethan's cabin for a snack.

I'd been satisfied playing in the boat in the field, but it was as if some kind of fever had come over Ethan. He couldn't stop talking about putting it in the water and having a *real* adventure. He worked on me non-stop and, just as he probably knew would happen, he finally wore me down.

It wasn't until I'd given in and we were on our way to get the boat that I thought of lifejackets. Specifically, that we didn't have any. I mentioned that to Ethan.

"You're just trying to back out on me," he accused. "Forget the lifejackets. We're not going out far enough to need them anyway."

"You can drown in a few inches of water," I said. I wasn't sure how, but that was something I'd heard my mom say.

"Why would you do that?" Ethan asked. "Why wouldn't you just stand up?"

I couldn't argue with the logic in that, so that was the end of the lifejacket discussion. By then, we'd reached the house where the boat was. We stopped talking as we slipped behind some bushes and snuck through to the back field where the shed was. We flipped the boat upright and slid it through the grass to the bank. Trying to ease it over the bank was a lot harder than it looked. We lost control and watched as the boat took off on its own with a quick plunge to the shore. Ethan scrambled down to it with me right behind him and we checked for signs of damage. It looked fine.

Pushing it the last few feet into the water was the hardest part but we kept at it until we got it in. Then we hauled our shoes off, tossed them into the boat and sloshed through the water to its side. Getting in took some effort but we hoisted ourselves over the side and into it after a few tries. I found myself in the bottom looking at an enormous spider in a huge web under the front seat.

"I'm older, so I sit in the front," Ethan announced.

He hadn't seen the spider and I didn't bother mentioning it. I moved out of his way, took the back seat, and grabbed my oar. It wasn't as easy paddling in the water but we pushed off and drifted a few feet away from land, which was as far as we'd agreed to go.

"There's a bit of water coming in but don't worry, that's normal," Ethan said. It was about the same time that I felt water underfoot. I grabbed my shoes before they got wet and sat them on the seat beside me.

"Are you sure?" I asked.

"Calm down, landlubber," he said with a sneer. "I've been in old fishing boats a couple of times and I remember one of the fishermen saying that they all take on a bit of the sea. Or something like that. Anyway, it's just a trickle."

I looked at the growing pool at my feet. "It's coming in kind of fast," I said.

"Don't worry, it'll stop in a couple of minutes," Ethan assured me.

Except, it didn't stop. It came in faster and faster, until even Ethan couldn't pretend we weren't going to have a problem if we didn't do something about it.

"We'll have to bail some out until it quits coming in," he said. He looked around like there might be a couple of pails handy, which obviously there weren't. Then his eyes rested on his shoes and he picked them out of the pool in the bottom of the boat and tossed one to me.

We used the shoes to scoop water out, but they didn't hold much and our arms couldn't work fast enough to keep up. No matter how frantically we bailed, the water level kept rising. What had started as an inch in the bottom was soon up around our ankles and there was no sign of it slowing down. By then, we both realized it was hopeless.

"We'll have to jump ship," Ethan declared.

"What about the boat?" I asked. "We can't just leave it here."

"Don't worry, nobody will know we took it," Ethan said. That was when his head came up and he took a good look around for the first time since we'd started bailing. The bravado disappeared in a flash and all the colour drained from his face.

While we'd been busy tossing water out of the boat with Ethan's shoes, the tide had also been busy. We'd been drawn a good stretch from shore.

"We're going to have to swim in," I said.

But Ethan's next words made it clear why his face had gone so white. "I can't swim," he said.

"You can't swim?" I didn't doubt him, but at the same time it seemed I was hearing something that couldn't be true.

He shook his head. "I'm going to drown out here."

"You're not going to drown," I said, trying to sound more confident than I felt. "We'll holler for help and keep bailing like crazy until someone comes."

"It's coming in faster by the minute," Ethan said. The terror on his face was awful.

Then I had an idea. "Maybe the water isn't even that deep," I said. "Let me see one of those paddles."

He passed it to me. I leaned over the side and stuck it down as far as I could reach but it didn't touch bottom. I couldn't look at Ethan.

"Help!" I yelled. "Somebody help us!" Ethan joined in and we yelled and bailed like mad. There was no sign that anyone had heard and I could see that Ethan was on the edge of complete panic.

This worried me a lot because I could see it wouldn't be long before the boat went completely under. I didn't know if I was a good enough swimmer to pull Ethan to shore, but if he was in a panic, it would be risky even to try. He could end up drowning both of us. I had to calm him down.

"Hey," I said, "Don't forget that your mom and dad have been in tighter spots than this and they got out all right. You can do it, too."

But Ethan turned to me, half dazed, and said, "My father's in jail. And I have no idea where my mother is."

I stared at him, stunned. "But, all the stuff you told me—"

"I made it up. My dad's what they call a career criminal and my mother took off years ago. She phones once in a while and tries to tell me she misses me."

I felt a jolt, which, for a second or two, I thought was shock from what he'd just told me. Then I realized it was the boat.

"We hit something!" I said.

"What do you mean?"

"We've run into a sand dune and got stuck— it's like a little hill underwater. See? We're not moving now."

It took a minute or two for Ethan to get it. We couldn't sink anymore—and he wasn't going to drown.

We got yelled at. A lot.

Well, first we got rescued. I don't know how long that took—it seemed we were standing in the boat with water up to our knees for hours, but it was probably a lot less than that. We were finally able to wave down a couple in a small boat that was passing by not too far away. When they got as close as they could without hitting the dune, I swam over and they hauled me in. I told them Ethan couldn't swim and the guy, who had a *lot* of muscles, swam over with a lifesaver and got him to the boat too.

They took us to a nearby wharf, called our folks and waited for someone to show up and claim us. That turned out to be my dad. He shook hands with both of them a couple of times and told them he could never repay them. They said anyone would have done the same and they were just glad Ethan and I were all right. Dad got their names and asked for their phone number. He said *he'd* be the one in danger if he went back to his wife without it.

We got in the car, then, and drove back to Schooner Point. Dad hardly got the car stopped before the doors were yanked open and we were yanked out. Mom got me and Gramps got Ethan. They nearly squeezed us to death and there were a whole lot of public kisses that I'd rather not talk about.

As soon as the hugging and kissing were over with, the yelling started. I got plenty but Ethan sure got his share, too.

"I've never been so upset in all my born days," Gram sobbed and yelled all at the same time. Gramps asked him if he was trying to kill his grandmother. They took turns telling him he was all they had left to care about in the world and they loved him more than life itself and he was never to do anything so foolish again and a whole lot of other things. I couldn't hear everything because my mom and dad were hollering stuff at me at the same time.

Then they took each of us to our own cabins and fed us.

I was feeling strange the next morning. It was as if the day before hadn't really happened, even though I knew it had. My brain was busier than it had ever been—jumping from one thing to another like an overactive cricket of some sort.

I stole a boat.

We could have drowned.

Ethan has no parents.

Ethan is a liar.

One thought that hadn't occurred to me yet was that we were going to have to go face the boat's owner and admit what we did. Well, it had sure occurred to my folks and Ethan's grandparents. First thing after breakfast Dad and Gramps marched us to the place we'd taken the boat from and knocked on the door.

I'd expected someone old, since the boat looked ancient, but the man who came to the door was younger than my dad. Soon as it swung open, Ethan spoke up.

"We took your boat and it sank," he said, "and we're real sorry."

"*Real* sorry, sir," I agreed.

"Call me Gavin," the man said. "I heard about the boat. Heard it could have ended a lot worse than it did, too."

"I almost drowned," Ethan agreed, though he'd never had so much as a mouthful of water.

"He would have taken me with him," I felt obliged to point out. "'Cause drowning victims panic."

Gavin nodded. "I'm glad neither of those things happened," he said.

"Well, young man, we owe you a boat, and we mean to make good on it," Gramps said.

"Forget it. It wasn't worth much," Gavin said.

"Because it sank?" Ethan asked.

"Well, not exactly," Gavin told him. "Those old lap strake boats leak if they're put in the water dry like that. They need to be wet down first, so the wood can swell and tighten. That's why it sank. I'm just glad it was the only thing that did."

So was I.

Dad and Ethan's Gramps did their best to talk Gavin into letting them pay him something for the boat but he kept refusing. Then it seemed he had an idea.

"How about we have the boys do some work to pay for it instead?"

"Now that's a fine idea," Dad said. "What did you have in mind?"

"Shades of Tom Sawyer," Gavin said with a smile. "I keep meaning to paint the old picket fence that goes around the property, but I never find the time."

We didn't say so, but that actually sounded like it might be fun to me and Ethan. Of course, that was before we spent two whole days at it. Even with Gavin pitching in and helping now and then, we only finished the part of the fence that ran along the front of the property after all that time. Our arms were nearly ready to fall off and I couldn't imagine many things that might smell worse than that paint.

Gavin came along to put everything away at the end of the second day. "You boys are really getting the hang of this," he said. "I bet you'll have the rest of it done in four or five more days, tops."

Ethan looked like he wished he'd drowned after all and I was too tired and sore to speak.

"Or—" Gavin paused. He seemed to be thinking. Then he said, "Instead of any more painting— what if you solemnly promised that you'd never take anything without permission again?"

"We *promise*!" Ethan and I yelled at the same time.

"Hold 'er now boys, this is serious. I want you to think hard about it. Because it's a commitment for the rest of your lives. You have to be sure that you'll be men enough to keep your word."

We thought hard, just like he said. And we were sure.

Theo was finally back! Ethan and I had been to his place looking for him a few times with no luck, but now, with just a couple of days left before we'd be leaving, there he was.

We raced up the bank, shouting and waving,

and he came out to the edge of his lawn and waited for us with a big smile on his face.

"It's me, Theo! I'm Adam!" I said when I reached him.

"Recognized your voice," he said, chuckling. "And you must be Ethan."

"Right!"

"Well, well. It's good to see you boys. You're a fine looking pair, I must say."

"Is it awesome being able to see again?" I asked.

"It's a blessing like nothing I can explain," he said.

We all went to the deck and sat down, though I was near bursting to show him the piece of driftwood we had for him. We'd brought it with us on one of the earlier trips when we were looking for him and instead of lugging it back and forth, we'd hidden it behind a big old tree stump to the side of his backyard.

I know it was silly, but I was expecting an extra great story out of it. It was the biggest and nicest piece of driftwood I'd brought there all summer.

It would have to wait a bit, though because Theo had something on his mind.

"I hear you boys hijacked an old clinker and sunk 'er," he said. "And nearly sunk yourselves at the same time."

"We were going to take it back," I said. I hated for Theo to think I was a thief.

"Yeah. We were just borrowing it," Ethan added.

"If you didn't *ask*, you didn't borrow it," Theo said. Apparently, he knew the whole darned story. "But what I want to know is: Were you afraid?"

"Real scared," I said.

"Not me," Ethan said.

Theo and I both turned to look at him.

"I was *terrified*," he finished.

"I see you learned something from it then," Theo said.

"I sure did. I'll never take anything that's not mine again."

"Good, good," Theo said. He smiled at Ethan. "That's important. But didn't you learn something else?"

Ethan didn't answer right away. When he did, his head dropped and he stared at the ground as he spoke.

"You mean about telling the truth, don't you?"

Theo nodded.

"Is that why you told us the story about that girl, Kiah, who made things up?"

"I told you the story the wood gave me," Theo said.

"It felt like it was about me," Ethan said.

"Our hearts hear the whispers they need to hear," Theo said. "If we are wise, we take them in."

"I tried not to—until the boat was sinking," Ethan said. He looked up again. "Then it felt like my last chance."

Since Ethan had been brave enough to tell

his story, I told them about Billy, and how the stories with the coyote and the fish had made me realize that I was the one who wasn't being a good friend, even though I'd tried to put the blame on him.

"I told him I'm sorry a couple of times, but it doesn't look like he's going to forgive me," I said. "I check every day and he won't answer my messages."

I felt a catch in my throat then, and decided it might be a good idea to change the subject.

"The piece of plank you told me to keep—I still never figured that out. Can you give me a hint?"

"Just as I told you before, it came to you for a reason," Theo said. I waited, but he didn't add anything else. After a bit, I told him we had a surprise for him. Ethan was closest to the tree stump where we'd hidden the new piece of driftwood, so he went and brought it over.

Theo took hold of it and sat admiring it for a few minutes. He turned it over and looked it up and down.

"This is a fine piece of driftwood," he said. "Thank you, boys."

"But, where is it from?" I asked. "Tell us the story!"

Theo's thin fingers moved along the lines of the wood, pausing here and there. He closed his eyes for a moment or two.

"I don't seem to know where this one came from," he said. He sounded sad, but there was no surprise in his voice.

"Has that ever happened before?" Ethan asked.

"Depends what you mean by 'before'," Theo said, "I never had the gift of seeing stories in the wood until I lost my sight."

Ethan and I exchanged worried looks.

"I might as well tell you boys that I think the gift is gone," Theo added. "I believe it left when I got my sight back."

"But, *why*?" Ethan asked.

"Why?" Theo chuckled. "I think you need a wiser man than me to answer that. If I was guessing, I'd say that there's a kind of balance, where if one thing is missing, something else fills its place, if you know how to find it."

"But, couldn't you have both things?" I said.

"I suppose that's possible, but it doesn't seem to be the case, at least not for me."

"What about the things you already saw?" I said. "Can you still see those stories?"

"It doesn't seem so," Theo said. "I wondered about that earlier, and tested it out. There wasn't so much as a hint of what I saw before."

He took another long look at the piece of driftwood in his hands, and said, "It may be that one kind of sight gets in the way of the other."

We let that sink in for a bit. Then I said, "It must be better to actually be able to see anyway, right?"

"Sight is a wonderful thing," Theo said. "But the main thing, as I see it, is to find the good in whatever your situation is. A person can miss out on a lot if they spend their days complaining about what they're missing, instead of appreciating what they have."

———

Ethan and his grandparents were already gone when Theo came to our cabin for supper the night before we left for home. After we'd eaten, he asked if he could look at Mom's paintings. It took a while because he flipped through the canvases slowly, examining each one carefully— and there were quite a few. Mom had been busy ever since she got her confidence back.

They were mostly local scenes from interesting points of view. The bay, trees, wildflowers, rustic homes—that kind of thing. Morning, afternoon and evening paintings, in different lights and weather conditions. I hadn't realized how many she'd finished. There were some close-ups of bugs and small animals, and a few with people at a distance. One was on the beach and I could tell it was me and Ethan, even though we were a long ways off and walking the other way.

"I'd like you to have a painting," Mom told Theo when he'd finished looking. "Please choose whichever one you want."

He thanked her, and thumbed through them until he came to a canvas that had been painted on a rainy evening as daylight was fading. It was dark and hazy with blurred images. He smiled.

"I'd like this one," he said.

Later, after we'd driven Theo back home, I heard Mom and Dad talking about the painting he'd chosen.

"You'd think he'd have wanted something bright and cheery," Mom said.

"Especially after all the years he lived in that kind of darkness," Dad agreed.

But I think I understood.

Unpacking the car when we got home didn't take as long as it had at Schooner Point. That was because this time we didn't have to sort it all out. We carried most of the stuff into the hallway and plunked it there for Mom to go through.

"I'll take it from here, men," she told me and Dad. "I have a system for unpacking. Besides, I need to burn off some energy after sitting in the car all that time."

I asked if it was all right for me to go to Billy's place and she said it was fine.

Billy had never answered my messages saying I was sorry for how I'd acted, so I was a bit nervous on the way there. But when I rounded the corner on his street, he was sitting out on his front step and when he saw me coming, his hand came up in greeting.

"Hi," he said as I crossed the yard toward him.

"Hey, Billy."

"When did you guys get back?"

"Just now. I came right over."

He didn't say anything to that, so I went ahead and plunged in. "I thought you might still be mad about the way I acted and everything."

"No, I'm not mad."

"I sent you a message to say I was sorry."

"Yeah. It's okay."

"I thought you were still mad—and that's why you never answered me."

"I wasn't mad. I just didn't feel like sending any messages."

"How come?"

Billy cleared his throat. Then he said, "Bailey died."

It had never once occurred to me that Bailey was really that sick, or that he might not make it. Billy looked about as busted up as I'd ever seen him.

"Aw, gee, Billy. I'm real sorry." It didn't seem like that was enough to say, but I couldn't think of anything else.

"I'm glad I was here to take care of him, and say goodbye to the old boy."

"You did the right thing," I said. "I shouldn't have given you a hard time about it. I feel real bad about it, and about Bailey."

Billy nodded. "I sure miss him," he said.

"He was a real good dog," I told him. Then I

shut up and just listened while he talked about some of the things Bailey used to do.

"He was the best," Billy said at the end. A tear ran down his cheek and he leaned forward and swiped it off with his hand. I pretended like I didn't know he was crying.

After a bit, he said he wanted to get out of there. I went with him to visit Bailey's grave, which he told me he'd dug himself. There wasn't much to do there, but we stood and looked at the mound of earth for a few minutes.

"I'm going to make a marker for him," Billy said.

"That'll be good, Billy," I said. "Bailey would like that. What are you going to make it out of?"

"My dad says I should paint a rock, but Bailey didn't like rocks." Billy said. "He liked fetching sticks, so I'm thinking I'll get a couple of pieces of deck lumber."

When we left Bailey's grave, we took a walk over to my house.

"Hey! Good to see you, Billy," Dad said. "How was your summer?"

"Bailey died," Billy said.

I could tell the way his head kind of jolted that Dad had forgotten Bailey was the name of Billy's dog.

"I'm sorry to hear that," Dad said. The question, *"Who is Bailey?"* was behind his words almost as clear as if he'd come right out and asked it. He turned and called, "June?"

Mom's head popped around the corner from where she'd been putting things away in the kitchen.

"Did you call me, dear?"

"Did you hear about Bailey passing away?" Dad asked.

Mom's face switched right away from a bit impatient to sad. She hurried down the hall and gave Billy a hug. "Oh, dear," she said. "That's awfully sad, Billy. I knew he was old but I didn't realize the end was that close for him. Did you have to have him put down?"

Dad finally got it. He told Billy he was sorry again. Then he leaned over a bit and ruffled Billy's hair. Because nothing cheers you up more than getting your head mauled.

We got out of there and went to my room. I showed Billy my piece of driftwood and told him all about the oak tree. I could see he was impressed the way he held the wood and looked it over as he listened.

Theo had told me that piece of wood came to me for a reason, and that was the moment I understood what the reason was.

"You think that piece of plank would be good enough for Bailey's grave?" I said.

Billy's eyes widened and he looked right at me. "For *real*?"

"It's yours, Billy."

"Thanks, Adam." He held it against himself like it was the greatest piece of wood in the world.

"This will be the best marker I could ever have hoped for."

"Let's drop it off at your place and take a walk," I suggested.

We did that, and then we wandered around a bit aimlessly until Patty Florence's place came into view, which was when Billy said, "We should see if Patty is home."

You could have knocked me down with a good puff of air. Billy, wanting to go visit a girl? On the other hand, I didn't mind the chance it gave me to bring up the twins. Especially Mackenzie. I'd had a friend request from her a few days after they left Schooner Point. Makayla, too, but Mackenzie's was first so that meant she'd been thinking about me.

"Sure," I said. "Patty's okay, I guess. And actually, I hung around for a few weeks with a couple of girls at Schooner Point. Twins. They were pretty cool."

Billy gave me a strange look.

"No reason a guy can't be friends with a girl—if she's okay I mean," I told him. Patty wasn't cool like the twins, that's for sure. But, who was I to judge Billy? If he wanted to hang out with her, I wasn't going to give him a hard time about it.

"Her dog had pups," Billy said, never taking his eyes off me. "Mom said I can have one when they're ready. What are *you* going on about?"

"Nothing. I was just saying." I felt my face getting a bit warm. "The summer sure went by fast, didn't it?"

Billy gave me another strange look but he let it go and a minute or two later we turned on the path to the Florence house. I could hear yipping through an open window before we got halfway to the door. Billy gave it a couple of good bangs with his fist and Patty's older sister opened it. She rolled her eyes.

"You again," she said. "Well, come on in, I guess."

She called for Patty, who came right along and led us to the room where the mother and pups were gathered on a big braided rug. There were five of them—chubby and cute and noisy as all get-out.

Billy didn't approach them. He dropped down onto his haunches and let his hands fall to his sides. "There's one of them that comes to me first almost every time," he said. His eyes burned with a kind of longing and I hoped whichever one he was talking about wouldn't disappoint him.

"Have you picked out which one you want yet?" Patty asked.

"Almost," Billy said.

I watched as three of the pups decided to head Billy's way, their tiny, pointed tails going a mile a minute as they made a dash in his direction. I felt a bit bad for him because they all got there at the same time.

But Billy's eyes must have been operating some kind of internal stop watch because he looked at me and said, "Did you *see*? He did it again—this guy almost always gets to me first." As he spoke, he scooped up a wriggling furball the colour of pulled toffee and pressed his face into it.

"Looks like he picked you, Billy," I said.

"I guess so," Billy said. "I'll just have to take the little rascal home."

His face was radiant.

You never have to guess what kind of mood Billy is in.

AN INTERVIEW WITH
VALERIE SHERRARD

Theo tells several folk tales that seem to be drawn from all around the world. Where did these stories come from?

The folk tales Theo tells are my inventions. In fact, that aspect of the story was the key factor that got me interested in writing Driftwood. I thought it would be wonderful to be able to create folk stories within the main story, and I loved the challenge of trying to give each of the tales a unique and authentic voice.

You have written picture books and teen novels as well as novels for younger readers. What do you like best about writing for middle-grade readers?

It was a lovely surprise to find how naturally my characters developed when I began writing for middle grade readers. I've felt connected to those characters in a deeper and different way than has been the case when writing for teens. No doubt this relates to the vulnerability of this age group.

Do you have a daily writing routine or do you just write when you feel particularly inspired?

Early in the morning and late at night are my best writing times – probably because they tend to offer the fewest distractions. I write pretty much every day. Sometimes it feels effortless, sometimes I work hard to get a few paragraphs on the page.

What are some of the greatest obstacles that a writer has to face? How do you overcome them?

There comes a point in almost every book I've written where I lose faith in the story – or rather, in my execution of the story. I've heard many writers speak of this experience as well, so I would encourage new writers to keep that in mind if that happens to them. The remedy is usually as simple as going back and reading what you've written right from the start.

Like Driftwood, your previous middle-grade novel, The Glory Wind, was also told from the perspective of a young boy. Where do you get your "young boy" voice? How are you able to identify with young boys so well?

I'm not entirely sure. I grew up with two brothers, and I raised a son, and fostered many adolescent boys, but I don't think that fully explains where the young boy voices come from. All I know for sure is that some of my favourite projects have been from the male perspective, and it's felt perfectly natural to write in those voices.

Have you ever stayed in a campsite like the one in Driftwood?

No I haven't. But Schooner Point and its cabins are real—and just a few minutes drive from my home. When I was considering a setting for this story, it seemed a good fit.

In Driftwood, Theo is visually impaired but then regains his sight. Is there a moral in that event that you hope readers will see?

Yes, definitely. Most of the time Theo leaves it to his audience to find meaning (friendship, loyalty, trust) in what he tells them – but he makes an exception and speaks openly about the lesson to be found in what he's lost and what he's gained.

ALSO BY VALERIE SHERRARD

TUMBLEWEED SKIES

"Sherrard writes with compassion and understanding about some tough issues, and her characters show remarkable depth. A realistic, moving story of how a broken family copes with loneliness and anger as they search for healing in their lives."
—*School Library Journal* **starred review**
Finalist for the Ann Connor Brimer Award for Children's Literature

THE GLORY WIND

"Luke's first-person narration is fresh and emotionally true, charting his growing awareness of his own human failure to live up to Gracie's tender yet believable goodness. This haunting depiction of small-mindedness will leave readers wondering, as Luke comes to, about Gracie's true nature: heavenly child–or angel?"
—*Kirkus* **starred review**
Finalist for the TD Canadian Children's Literature Award and the CLA Children's Book of the Year for Children; winner of the Ann Connor Brimer Award for Children's Literature and the Geoffrey Bilson Award for Historical Fiction.